From Dusk to Dawn

A Collection of Short Stories

Joe Chilson

This is a work of fiction. Names, characters, places and incidents either are products of the author's imagination or are used fictitiously. Any resemblance to actual events or locales or persons, living or dead, is entirely coincidental.

CONTENTS

INTRODUCTION

This collection has been a long time in the making in some form or the other. I first started trying to write a collected work of stories as a part of my high school creative writing class, but I always found myself doubting my ability to deliver the intended detail necessary to convey the full picture.

In writing the fourteen stories contained here, I sought to break down some of the walls between what is considered "traditional storytelling." You'll find that, although each story conveys a varying genre and theme, each seeks to arise some degree of emotional appeal. In doing so, I believe I've crafted some of the darkest stories to ever escape my imagination, as well as a few that simply seek to entertain.

I will advise that some of the themes included in the works that follow may illicit an uneasiness in some, while others also touch on topics that some might deem sensitive in nature. I even found myself questioning the line between reality and fiction at times, and I hope they succeed at conveying that same level of disillusion in reading them.

Before we dive right into it, I want to offer a few words of thanks to several individuals who played a role in ensuring I saw this project to completion. Firstly, out of those who glimpsed the earliest drafts of the stories catalogued here, Justin Costello and Elizabeth Lester provided constructive criticism and words of encouragement almost every step of the way. I also owe a considerable gratitude to Katie Valliere, who kept the cover art from looking like a middle school PowerPoint presentation slide. (Her words, not mine.) If not for the sizable support I received upon announcing my intentions to publish, I'm not sure I would have ever maintained the focus necessary to finish what I started.

And of course, to every reader willing to embark on this journey with me, I'd also like to thank you for giving my book a chance. That's all any writer could ask for.

Now, with all the formalities out of the way, I hope you enjoy your time here in my imagination.

Dusk

Thunder rumbled solemnly in the distance. The ashen clouds overhead briefly flickered to life as foreboding silhouettes of pending doom. These dreadful omens punctuated the fleeting moments of their final days, with the last flecks of sand draining from eternity's hourglass.

The family huddled together, clinging to what little warmth the dying embers of their fire still provided them, as the sky itself seemed to voice displeasure at the outcome of human affairs. Those lightly flickering cinders were all that remained of a fallen civilization. The world itself crumbled slowly around them, and still they clung to one another as fractured pillars, themselves fated to crumble.

The nations of the world cast their lots in the days leading up to this. They fought for control, each justified in their cause, until not but a cascade of destruction lingered in their wake. This penultimate climax spread worldwide, reaching the shores of every continent, until even Mother Nature herself turned traitor. What remained thereafter were the scorched remains of countless civilizations, churned out by their own double-edged sword.

Now, look upon this one meager and powerless family, with the clock ticking ever closer to their final moments. The light and warmth fades from the ashes strewn before them, and so too are their own souls laid barren as empty husks without reason. These bystanders played no role of importance in the falsehoods that brought them over that precipice, and yet they share the same fate as those generals, marching their troops along the blood-soaked trenches of the final crusade.

Time and time again, through the history of the human condition, the people of the world find themselves bound by a thin strand of fate. Now, those fibers grow thin and tattered. This end, long foreshadowed, belongs to all who walk beneath that shared sky. None will escape this loosely bound disparity.

The dying flame lit upon the face of a father who knows the truth. His two children sit on either side of him, shivering and desperate for the days of warmth.

Henry was alone with the children now. His wife, Meredith, drew her last breath seven days prior. She contracted what they regarded as "The Sickness." He could see her still, in his mind's eye, as her body convulsed and twisted in ways that seemed humanly impossible. The memory of her screams lingered with him even in the face of his own impending death.

The pollution that spread, as the final wave of the last great battle drew to a close, carried The Sickness in its wake. Those in the vicinity of the booming concerto that ushered the fall of man contracted The Sickness before the greater populace grew wary of its looming threat. Soon, a murky miasma reached even peaceful shores, and a relentless spree of suffering befell those most susceptible to the toxin. Those afflicted were ravaged by painful fits, and their bodies contorted and disintegrated in on themselves. They always welcomed death's cold embrace in the end.

The children were twelve and fifteen respectively. Mary, the eldest, stayed by her mother's side, even in her final hours, but Jonathan fled the scene, incapable of recognition. Like Henry, his son chose ignorance over cruel reality; they clung onto the faintest glimmer of hope hanging on the horizon.

They were both misguided in their optimism. Reality stood before them as a bald reminder.

In the end, Meredith had been reduced to a warped and skeletal figure. The Sickness got the better of her. No misguided prayers could divert her fate, just as mankind's great ambitions led only to these dimly lit halls, where only despair lived and thrived.

Rising from their encirclement around the fire, Henry moved toward the door that housed the pantry. Their supplies were thinning now, adding to their troubles. Soon they would find themselves at risk of starvation, in addition to exposure to the toxic fallout. The thought of starving to death seemed almost as frightening in its own way.

He returned to them with a can of creamed corn, which he prepared over the fading heat of their makeshift fire. The warmed tin canister passed from person to person, with each only eating enough to drive their pangs of hunger back into hibernation. Even the youngest knew they were only delaying the inevitable.

They always ate in silence. No one had much to say anymore; the act of speaking itself seemed almost cumbersome.

Overhead, the sky grumbled discontentedly, as forked streaks of lightning drove earthward. It was like something straight out of the Book of Revelations, except there were no trumpets sounding to herald them into the nether.

Before turning in for the night, on bare mattresses that lay strewn upon the floor, the three shared an embrace. They clung to one another, each awash in their own individualized fears. The weight of the day poured off them. This was the only time they felt truly united as a family. Those moment were fleeting, however.

On that night in particular, Henry found himself tossing and turning, finally coming to rest upon his back. He looked skyward through the webbed cracks in what remained of their home's upper story. A faint rumbling vibration ran its course through the floor beneath his mattress. Sitting bolt upright, anticipating the next reverberation, he felt uneasy.

He could hear his children's labored breathing on either side of him. They were sleeping soundly, but their dreams were restless, reflecting the state of their subconscious.

Sitting there in the dark, he waited for those familiar vibrations to resound once more, yet all seemed still, almost uncomfortably so. He hoped the anxiety he felt was nothing more than a shadow cast in his mind, but a part of his inner awareness knew better than to believe that.

He laid back in hopes of getting some sleep himself. It took some time, but at last he felt himself drifting off. He saw Meredith in his dreams, and she was as she had been before this rotten affair began. He felt at peace there, holding onto a version of his wife yet to find herself embroiled in pain and madness, with only the slightest hint of his own trepidation wallowing in the corner. It almost made him forget the truth of the matter for a time.

Then reality came screeching back into the forefront.

By sunrise the next morning, the tremors had returned and intensified tenfold. Henry nearly slept through them, entrapped by his own hopeful imaginings. Then the earth began to split, and he hardly had a chance to return to his senses in time to realize what was happening.

A deep black crevice opened in the floor, and Henry only had enough time to gather himself and his oldest child, before the ruins of their home came crashing down around them. He and Mary escaped nearly unscathed.

Jonathan had not been so lucky.

An avalanche of their every worldly possession plummeted downward into that seemingly bottomless abyss. Henry imagined he could hear Jonathan's screams reverberating upwards, as he fell deeper and deeper into the bowels of the Earth. Perhaps it had been nothing more than his mind playing tricks on him, but there was no denying his son's untimely demise.

It took a great deal of restraint to keep Henry from jumping in after him, deluded by the notion that maybe—just maybe—he could still turn the tables. Realization socked him in the gut without remorse, and he fell to his knees there at the edge of the crevice. It swallowed the remnant of their home in one wide gulp, now standing as a puckered blemish upon the face of this ruined world. His face dropped into his open hands, and the fresh stream of tears felt scalding.

Henry's trembling daughter stood behind him on what remained of Maple Avenue. Her eyes were wide and delirious. She was both seeing and not seeing the tragedy laid bare before her. She wanted to believe she were still asleep and dreaming, but the logical part of her mind spoke up and advised otherwise. Mary peered into the depths, bewildered by the thought of her brother's underground tomb. It seemed almost too much for her mind to bear.

Her father knelt on the cracked asphalt before her. His heart had been pulled asunder once more. The loss of Meredith left him with an unsettling loneliness that only grew satiated by the necessity to take responsibility for the well-being of their children. Now he failed even at this. His mind quickly spiraled downward into an inescapable pit of despair.

The final days were upon them, and already they were reduced by half.

"How do we go on like this?" His words were muffled behind his hands. They were the solemn words of a broken man. "There's nothing left for us."

It felt like only yesterday they were all seated around the dinner table, swapping stories from their mundane lives, without so much as a worry in the world. Six months had passed since the world started into its death throes, with ripples of ceaseless chaos spiraling outward from its epicenter, and yet, within his loss addled mind, it all seemed to blur together into one single, maddening day.

A small hand seemed to extend from across a great distance to pull upon the tattered sleeve of his shirt. His daughter was trying to pull him back together, to get him to snap back from the brink of destruction. He ignored her and surrendered to his baser instincts.

Then came another tug, this one more insistent than the last. "Dad?" Mary's voice sounded distant and unfamiliar as it reached his ears—in another world perhaps. "Dad, I think we'd better get away from here." How unexpected for his fifteen-year-old daughter to become the voice of reason amidst this catastrophe.

Henry bore no concept of time passing around him. Every clock in the world might as well have broken the second Jonathan succumbed to the Earth's wrath. Nearly an hour had passed with them bearing witness to the aftermath, until his daughter's frightened voice finally reached him. He slowly regained his sense of the moment.

He was breathing heavily, with a light-headed sense of weightlessness enveloping him. He opened his mouth to speak in response to her pleas, and his voice came out sounding rough around the edges. "No, sweetie." He tried to sugarcoat it, but he came off sounding only bitter. "There's nowhere left for us to go. We're going to die here." It seemed what little hope stayed with Henry, even after his wife's passing, would die with Jonathan. His surrender to death signaled an end to his struggle.

Mary's eyes were filling with tears now. Henry never turned to look at her, but he could hear the fear and desperation in his voice all the same. "Don't say that…We can't just stay here. We have to at least try." Her insistence and will to persevere stood in bold contrast to his resignation.

Henry's head drooped slowly, until his chin came to

rest upon the flat of his chest. "I don't know what to do anymore. I can't keep going on like this."

"How could you say that?" Her voice rose to a shrill cry, cutting away at his protests before they could dampen her determination. She bent and reached for his hand. He must have sensed her intentions, because just as she were about to grasp his larger hand in hers, he snapped it away without remorse. A certain coldness conveyed itself through this gesture, and it left Mary momentarily at a loss for words.

She would find her voice again, but when she did, her words lashed from the tip of her tongue, intending to cut deep. "This isn't what they would have wanted. They would have wanted us to keep going. We're supposed to be a family, and I know they wouldn't have just given up like this."

Her words seemed to weigh upon him, settling heavily upon his shoulders. He slumped further forward, shrinking away from her.

She waited, and when he still failed to respond, she settled upon her decision. "Fine, be that way." Turning on her heels then, she breathed deep and took off running from the edge of the crater. She left her father there, wallowing in self-pity.

It took Henry a second to realize what just happened. His eyes bulged and widened; understanding gave way to panic. Gathering his footing, he spun to watch Mary weaving her way down the avenue, being careful to steer clear of any obstacles in her path.

Thunder boomed overhead. Billowing storm clouds were moving in on the horizon, blotting out the fiery red ball that was the sun as seen through a heavy film. Lightning cascaded downwards at jagged angles, and it almost seemed to strike home several miles away.

He gave himself only a moment to regard these things

in accordance to his daughter's flight, before he took off running himself. His legs were shaky and apt to betray him, yet he urged himself onward.

Mary showed no signs of stopping. The lumbering hulks of the other homes that once occupied this quiet neighborhood blurred passed. She seemed altogether unfazed by the exertion.

"Mary, please stop," he called between labored breaths. He found himself struggling to maintain that brisk pace, but he knew if he stopped even for a second, she would pull too far ahead for him to ever hope to catch up.

She never slowed, not even at the recognition of his words carried across the distance.

Pushing himself well beyond his limit, Henry thought his lungs might explode from his chest. The distance between them grew smaller and smaller. His feet ground down upon the crumbling stretch of road. He wheezed and panted, fully aware that his strength would give out before long.

Through some miracle, he actually managed to catch up. Leaping forward, putting all his remaining strength into that last stride, he managed to wrangle her writhing form into his arms. She seemed desperate to evade capture. They were both momentarily airborne for an instant, as he tackled her to the ground, grasping her tight against his heaving chest.

Just then, the ground gave another lurch beneath them. An extensive gash formed in the asphalt.

They never stood a chance. Before either realized what was happening, a deep ravine opened along that stretch of Maple Avenue, swallowing them down into its dark embrace.

Faceless Gallery

Interrogation Room B

They had him right where they wanted him, or so they believed. Instances of premature congratulations were all too common, often leading to disappointment when the cards failed to land in their favor. Yet this instance seemed all but assured.

On the other hand, Catherine Henson retained a disposition of cautious disbelief. In matters of guilt, especially in regards to a case as heinous as the one seated before them, it seemed best to retain a touch of skepticism. The man in question, a thirty-four-year-old business owner from the city's outer rim, seemed the most likely perpetrator in the murder and mutilation of a young woman, whose remains turned up inside a dumpster not far from the suspect's apartment.

Grainy surveillance footage of that dimly lit back alley placed the accused in the vicinity of the body within the estimated window of time in which the woman's remains were deposited. Catherine remained on the fence, even with evidence to back their claims. As it happened, the footage also showed others coming and going around the same time, while the actual crime occurred off camera. Yet somehow, the precinct's up-and-coming rookies (Catherine regarded them as nothing but ill-mannered pups) leapt at the first sign of guilt. They mistakenly clung to the assumption that their initial suspect—who never received so much as a parking ticket in his life—bore all the trimmings of a killer.

She refused to believe it.

Therein lies the problem with the present state of law

enforcement in Ravenswell. The younger generation was too quick to point fingers and jump at the first sign of an obvious conclusion. From their perspective, every citizen hid the potential for evildoing just beneath the surface, and it was only a matter of time before their true colors came to light. True innocence existed only in fairy tales and bore little importance in their day-to-day routine.

Catherine, on the other hand, learned from the best. She knew better than to believe their misguided notions, often relying on nothing more than a gut feeling. Her fortieth birthday approached and loomed on the foreseeable horizon. She shared very little in common with these wide-eyed hopefuls, most of whom were only in their twenties.

The Chief of the Ravenswell City Police Department—who Catherine long regarded as a friend above all else—called upon her that morning with some concerns of his own. Howard Tristram grew up with Catherine's father. They thought themselves two lone gunslingers, serving side-by-side in the trenches, with crime growing ever more apparent on the streets they sought to protect. Catherine's father ducked out early, however, before they could truly establish everlasting order amidst the chaos.

"I think it should be you, Catherine." Howard's words conveyed an air of importance. "We can't afford to screw this up. Have you been reading the papers? The public is turning against us. We've made too many rash decisions as of late, and we're losing the trust of the people. We have to turn this around."

"You already know how I feel." Her tone made her sound older. She never let pass the opportunity to speak her objections for how many of their fellow officers chose to conduct themselves in the line-of-duty. She could see Howard's and her father's legacy quickly fading as these youngsters took center stage.

The chief nervously wiped at his lips with one meaty hand, as if trying to wipe away the bad taste that lingered there. "I know, I know, but I'm starting to think they're actually onto something this time."

"What changed your mind?" She quirked an eyebrow at him. His change of heart piqued her curiosity. Howard's judgement often shone more accurate than he cared to admit, and over the years, she developed an unshakable trust in him. He knew the field with certainty; that experience granted him an unmatched depth of insight.

"You just have to see him for yourself. The boys have him down in Interrogation Room B. There's something different about this one, Cat. It's something I can't put my finger on, but there's something not right about him." He sounded nervous. Catherine could never remember Howard showing even the slightest hint of hesitation, but it lingered in his every word now. "Please just do it for me." He asked her this not as her superior but as her friend.

She would go along with his ploy, of course. After everything Howard had done for her over the years, granting his request came as a no-brainer. Yet his nervous disposition set her mind on edge.

Thirty-minutes later, his insistence found Catherine standing on one side of a two-way mirror, observing a bald man, who seemed unconcerned with his current predicament. A pair of handcuffs encircled his wrists. She found him seated at the far side of a table; a vacant chair stood nearest the window, pushed neatly beneath the tabletop.

She sized him up, trying to observe the same traits that drew the chief's concern. The suspect's eyes seemed strangely youthful for his age; they were not unlike the eyes of a child. Stranger still, those eyes were looking right at her, as if observing her through the pane of glass. The design of the mirrored window made it so visualization occurred only from one side. It seemed ridiculous, but his eyes seemed to follow her every movement.

The chief and the interrogating officer were elsewhere, under the guise of discussing any potential breaks in the case. In actuality, Catherine knew this to be a plot, allowing her some time alone with the suspect.

A faint smile touched the suspected killer's lips. That smile seemed warm and almost understanding of her situation. "I know you're there," he spoke suddenly into the empty room. The mirror between them muffled the sound of his voice, but she could hear him all the same. "I can't see you, but I can feel you." He sounded confident and unshaken.

Caught off guard, she glanced back at the door. A part of her hoped the chief would choose that moment to return.

The man's steely gray eyes gazed upon her all the while. "Yes, I suspect your friends will be coming back very soon. I get the feeling they don't like me very much," he spoke again.

"Why would they like you?" she thought this to herself, not daring to speak the words aloud. *"They think you're a murderer, and I'm beginning to think they might be right."*

"I'm interested in knowing what you think of me." His smile widened. For a second, she believed him capable of reading her mind. "You're different. You see things others can't. You try to hide it, but it's as clear as day."

Just then, the door to the hall swung open. The chief stepped inside, with the interrogating officer following close behind. "I suspect everything is in order here?" the chief asked upon entry. He offered a less-than-discreet wink in her direction. "Now, Officer Lenahan, you'd best get this interrogation on the road. Report to me immediately if you should learn anything of interest." Then to Catherine: "Come, let's take a walk." She turned to him. Her face seemed drained of all color.

Officer Lenahan, a twenty-five-year-old man with short raven-colored hair, a freckled face, and the glassy-eyed look of a deer in the headlights, hastened to begin the interrogation. His attempts would prove fruitless.

The chief knew only something of great concern could rattle Catherine to this extent; it troubled him and hastened their departure.

Catherine followed the chief out into the hall. She chanced a glance back over her shoulder as they left. The bald man's smile projected some higher knowledge. It made her question everything she thought she knew of the constructs of guilt and innocence.

The chief's suspicions were substantiated now. Catherine knew something was very wrong about the man seated in Interrogation Room B.

The Man Behind the Smile

"His name is Stewart Perkins," Chief Howard Tristram told her, as they marched down the hall leading back to his office. "You see what I mean now? He makes your hair stand on end just looking at him."

Catherine nodded slowly, mostly to herself, but partly in agreement. She found herself drifting in and out of her own thoughts, only partly aware of their surroundings. The encounter continued playing on repeat in her mind. Stewart Perkins' words resound with increasing clarity.

"You're different." He sounded entirely convinced. *"It's as clear as day."*

What had he seen in her? How had she gained his interest in those few moments they spent together? It troubled her, touching the depths of her person in a way nothing ever had before. Stewart Perkins weaseled his way under her skin, just as he likely intended. Caught in his enchantment, Catherine failed to notice the slowly enclosing snare.

"Catherine?" The chief's words lured her back to reality. His eyes, brimming with concern, noted her vacant expression. They were standing outside the door to his office now. He leaned in closer, trying to read the lines on her face. "I think you checked out for a minute there. Are you okay?"

She pondered her own mental wellbeing for a moment before acknowledging his concerns with a response: "Sorry, I was just lost in thought for a minute there."

"You were thinking pretty hard, I'd say. What troubles you? Your face, it's so pale. I don't think I've ever seen you like this before." His lips pursed tightly. He never let his gaze waver. "If it has anything to do with the case, then I think you'd best spill the beans. It's better to work things out together. We are a team, after all." That made her smile, just the ghost of a smile, but a smile all the same.

The chief had known Catherine for most of her life. He knew the inner workings of her mind. His admiration for her distinct rationalization formed the cornerstone of their relationship. He felt he could trust her above all else.

"You know how it is these days. They all think of this as nothing more than another game of cops and robbers on the playground. You're cut from a different cloth, Catherine; you share your father's passion. I'd like to know what your gut is telling you," he pressed her, encouraging dialogue between them.

They entered the secluded confines of his office. He let the door snick closed. The chief walked around behind his desk, lowering his heavy frame into the well-worn seat.

Stewart Perkins' words continued echoing off the walls of her brain. The chief's distinct regard for her made them stand out with deepening emphasis.

The chief stayed patient, awaiting her response. He sat with hands clasped together over a mountain of overdue paperwork. He maintained a fatherly calm.

"I'm starting to think you were right," Catherine's words served as confession. "Something seems off about him."

"Did he say something to you?" Chief Tristram's brow drew together.

She glanced at him questioningly. "You know I didn't go in. I only just got a look at him."

The chief's head bobbed its agreement. "I know that, but the boys say he has a way of knowing when you're watching. They've asked him about it, and he only claims he can 'feel' their presence...It makes no sense to me, but they swear it's the truth."

"In that case..." Catherine hesitated, mulling over her thoughts in an attempt to find the right line of discourse. "He did say something, but it didn't make much sense. I didn't want to say anything, thinking it might make me sound crazy, but he told me I'm 'different'...Whatever that's supposed to mean..." Catherine heaved a sigh; she felt a tension unclenching in her chest. "I get the feeling we may be dealing with a touch of crazy. Nothing good ever comes from the ones that run off at the mouth like that."

Crazy seemed wrong, somehow. To her, Stewart Perkins was something else entirely.

Howard Tristram hung his head. "I feared as much...Your shared diagnosis only strengthens my assessment. Thank you, Catherine. I knew I could count on you."

Those words would haunt him for the rest of his days.

Knowing Eyes

Catherine spent the night that followed tossing and turning. Her thoughts seemed fated to turn rebel against her. Sleep lingered just out of reach, occupying the small quadrant of her mind not already desperately analyzing the events of the day.

Any time her eyelids should begin to droop in the slightest, that man would appear out of the darkness. His youthful, gray eyes peered back at her from the depths of her mind. They saw her coming unwound.

His eyes, at first glance, seemed devoid of the burdens of modern society, but just below the surface, they held secrets they would never yield willingly. They belonged both to a visage of childlike curiosity and to a craven who knows the truth behind all lies.

Seeing them lingering there, never relenting, his words came to her once more: *"I know you're there...I can't see you, but I can feel you..."*

Remembering his voice left her trembling and afraid.

She knew it seemed crazy—he was locked up in a cell, after all. Yet somehow, she could feel his eyes following her even now. His gaze peeled back the layers of her personage. That thought frightened her even more than the accusations laid at his feet.

Then, the words that remained unspoken between them: *"I know your deepest secrets, Catherine...You can't hide them from these eyes. They've seen more than you could ever imagine, and now they've seen you, too."* Those words lingered in the air, like the far-off hum of some untapped electrical current.

She huddled beneath the covers, clinging to some small semblance of security.

Behind those eyes, Catherine sensed an unspoken knowledge. Their owner claimed to behold some deeper potential within her. Now she found herself questioning her every decision leading up to this point.

In that moment, she settled upon a singular course of action. She would need to speak with him once more. As dawn bloomed on a new day, the illuminating convergence of their two conflicting ideals seemed inevitable. She petitioned herself to accept only truth and none of the gray matter between. Only then would she find peace once more.

Set upon this decision, her mind felt eased of its burden. Sleep rose to congratulate her, entombing her within its shallow embrace.

All the while she slept, those knowing eyes stayed unrelenting in their duty. They watched from across an unbridgeable expanse, as a crooked smile touched the lips of a jailbird taking flight.

Absolution

"I'm sorry, Catherine, but it's just not possible." The chief stood firm in his resolve.

That morning's first order of business saw Catherine crossing the threshold into the chief's office, prepared to take a stand on her involvement in the case. She needed to confront Stewart Perkins once more, just to get to the bottom of everything.

"You know it's in your best interest to let me in on this, Sir." She rolled out the formalities in trying to sway the conversation in her favor. She hoped years of fighting the good fight together would also bear influence on his decision. "Just let me meet him face to face. You won't regret it."

The chief laced his fingers together ponderously. His gaze seemed heavy, with a hint of remorse. That look appeared uncharacteristic amidst his usual stoic artifice. "No, Catherine, you don't understand. I'm afraid I really can't grant your request. My hands were tied in this. We had no choice but to turn the suspect loose this morning."

Catherine's face froze in an expression of awed disbelief. She wanted to believe she had simply misheard him. "What did you say?"

"The actual culprit—a troubled teen, already mixed up with a record of violence—turned himself in and confessed to the murder. He came into the station late last night, seeking protection in exchange for information. He found himself mixed up with the wrong crowd. They were looking for him, and he had nowhere else to turn." The chief heaved a tired shrug. "I'm sorry, kid, but it looks like we were wrong." He sounded unconvinced.

Catherine knew the law and what they needed to do in this situation, but that did little in brightening her outlook. They both knew better than to accept this.

Without another word, Catherine spun on her heels and stormed out. The door clattered shut behind her. The chief watched after her, failing to verbalize his wish to halt any further meddling on this front. He felt powerless in the face of Catherine's unwavering determination. They both knew the now free man bore an unseemly mark, yet they could progress no further down that path without any proof of wrongdoing.

Catherine hastened back to her own cubical-sized office. She pondered this outcome and the potential for added suffering in the wake of their ignorance. She considered the possibilities, seeking a more reasonable explanation.

As a steady stream of conspiracy flooded her brain, Catherine surveyed her office. Something caught her eye, halting her overactive synapses. A sealed envelope sat upon one corner of her desk. Her name shone in a meticulous hand, etched upon its ivory surface.

Even before examining its contents, she knew her troubles were only just beginning.

Answers

The envelope contained a handwritten note. Catherine recognized the address scrawled on the slip of paper. Their records reflected that same address as Stewart Perkins' last known residence.

Still, she wondered how that note found its way onto her desk. Is it possible he managed to slip unscathed from police custody, only to return for the sake of hand-delivering this message? It seemed absurd. The personal invitation only served in raising her suspicions.

Catherine saw herself as the unsung hero. She felt a strong desire to prove her deductions. For this, she would need to stay one step ahead of his devilish schemes— whatever they may be.

Deciding to tell no one of the breadcrumb trail laid out for her to follow, Catherine left the station that afternoon. Her firearm lay concealed beneath the flap of her jacket, resting at her hip. The gun served as a ward of sorts, against the evil she sought to unveil.

Consumed by the heat of the moment, Catherine succumbed to her own distinct madness. Her intended course saw her descending into the heart of the lion's den. Stewart Perkins already proved himself a formidable foe, perhaps even the most adept mover amidst the shadows. Driven to seek the truth, her curiosity took precedence even over fearing for her life.

She hardly regarded the distance between the station and his doorstep. Standing there, at the foot of the two-story apartment complex Stewart Perkins called home, her mad endeavor reached a penultimate turning point.

She considered turning back. The thought of burying her suspicions seemed all the more inviting in that moment. The questions would stay unanswered, but she thought she could push them down into the deepest recesses of her mind, never to be heard from again.

Except she would never forgive herself for letting this one slip if what she suspects proves true. Instead, she pressed a button on the callbox next to the door—the one labeled 2A. His name stood out in bold letters beneath the apartment number.

She held her breath for what felt like an eternity. A persistent certainty half convinced her that no one would answer, but just as she considered calling it quits, a curt and unfamiliar voice cut through the jagged hum of static issuing forth through the box's built-in speaker. "Come on up. I've been expecting you." His voice sounded different, but the underlying tone stayed the same. It made her skin crawl.

The door's electronic locked disengaged with a metallic clunk. Startled by the sound, she could feel her heart hammering away inside her chest. Swinging the door inwards, she mounted the stairs; they seemed to ascend endlessly. The sensation of trudging into enemy territory became almost palpable.

A cacophony of questions rattled around in her brain, touching the very foundation of her being. The repetition of those inquiries seemed bent on driving her to the brink of insanity, and maybe then she would truly understand what she read there in Stewart Perkins' knowing gaze.

Standing before a worn wooden door, accentuated by an engraved silver placard that read "2A", Catherine grew hesitant once more. Her pulse quickened as she raised her fist to knock. The motion seemed sluggish and delayed. The air itself seemed to weigh heavily on her. No sooner had her knuckles rapped upon the door, issuing forth a low, dry sound, before it began slowly creaking open, seemingly of its own volition. Light streamed through the building crack along the jamb of the door.

She stood frozen, waiting for him to emerge at any second. Nothing from all her years of experience prepared her for this. She found herself reverting into the mind-frame of a sniveling child, reduced to tears across the knee of a stern father figure.

Still standing in statuette form, she realized her fears were yet unfounded. No one emerged from the open door. Slowly, her senses snapped back to full attention. That uncertain moment bled into a brief, puzzling respite. She knew she needed to make the first move. With caution, she inched the door further inward, using only the tips of her fingers.

The light issuing forth from within grew brighter, until it illuminated a perfectly ordinary sitting room beyond. Nothing seemed immediately out of the ordinary. Stepping carefully, she scanned her surroundings with an eye for detail. Nothing of importance jumped out at her initially. The focal point of the room was a big screen television, mounted upon the far wall, with a well-worn leather loveseat sitting adjacent. These signs of normalcy calmed her nerves on entry.

After having crept across the mundane sitting room, she passed beneath an archway into the apartment's inner-fold. There she noted some strange décor strewn across the walls, situated just out of sight from the main entrance. A series of newspaper clippings hung there. Some were yellowed and faded with the passage of time, while others seemed pristine.

She intentionally left the front door open behind her, providing the option for a hasty escape; she glanced back that way now. As she weighed her options, her hand dipped to the steel holstered at her hip, reminding herself of its presence. Channeling its strength, a renewed sense of calm washed through her.

Stepping closer to the makeshift tapestry, her eyes moved from one clipping to the next. Dawning realization grew into full-blown terror. Each bold-faced headline jumped off the page at her. "Lincoln Stabber Still on the Loose— Fourteen Dead." Sidestepping to read the next, this one detailed the involvement of the Hampton Bomber; this still unidentified individual orchestrated an attack that leveled a small-town shopping mall. One after the next, each article recounted various acts of senseless cruelty—a few of which were well over a hundred years old. Some of the most heinous unsolved crimes in human history were preserved here, like exhibits in some twisted museum.

A second too late, Catherine heard footsteps approaching from behind. Before she could turn, the blunt end of a cast-iron skillet levered itself against the back of her head. She dropped to the floor as a momentary flash of pain debilitated her. A low groan permeated the silence, and the warm trickle of blood spread to the nape of her neck. Crumpled into a heap, her eyes struggled to focus on the form of her attacker towering over her.

As her vision cleared, the man's features grew increaseingly apparent. His jawline bore an angular slant, while the jovial fullness of his cheeks stood in strong opposition. His clothes—a pair of blue jeans and a white undershirt, with an apron that read "Kiss the Cook" tied around his neck— seemed too big for his slender frame. He wore his hair in a ponytail, and the golden hue almost seemed to cast a halo in the overhead light.

She failed to recognize any similarity between this man

and Stewart Perkins, until she glimpsed his eyes. They were a muted gray, and they seemed to acknowledge her with a touch of disdain.

He fell upon her, dropping his full weight, and before she could take defensive measures, her hands were yanked and tightly bound behind her back. Groveling at his feet, her eyes were alight with fearful anger, mostly in regards to her own stupidity. "Who are you?" she asked him, without ever letting the gallery of unidentified perpetrators slip from the forefront.

"Don't you recognize me?" He sounded amused.

She did recognize him on some level. The eyes were a dead giveaway. Yet, she remained skeptical of the possibility. How could he have changed so much since last they met?

She noticed his feet were bare, explaining his stealthy approach. His weapon of choice had momentarily been abandoned to allow the intricate handywork that resulted in the knotted length of nylon rope entangling her wrists. He reclaimed the blunt instrument soon after, and now stood poised, as if ready to strike once more.

Leaving her lying there momentarily, she heard him closing and latching the front door. He returned to hunker down beside her. "You see it now, don't you?" he asked, noting the roundness of her eyes. He took great interest in the first flicker of fear that lit on one's face, considering himself something of an expert on the subject. "I've been hunted since before you were even born, and yet here you are, thinking you're different from all the rest."

Catherine held her tongue. As hopeless as it seemed, she found herself holding onto the faint glimmer of hope that some opportunity for escape may still present itself.

"You almost had me, too," he told her, seeming almost enthralled at the thought. "You didn't know it at the time, but you almost hooked the biggest fish of all. It may have been nothing but luck, or maybe more a matter of being in the wrong place at the wrong time, but you almost had me all the same." His smile widened. "I was innocent this time around—believe it or not. The young man who gave himself over to your dogs is the true culprit, but I'm sure you already realize this has not always been the case."

"Who are you really?" she asked through clenched teeth. She sought to buy herself some time. If she could keep him talking long enough, someone from the station might take notice of her absence. The envelope containing his address lies open upon her desk even now. She only hoped someone would find it before he slipped the noose once more.

"I left my collection out for you to see." His eyes drifted upwards to admire the arrangement of newspaper clippings. "It's only a taste of my full collection, but I thought you would appreciate it."

Her dumbfounded expression said it all.

"I can't quite remember how long it's been," he went on. "Two-hundred years? Maybe three-hundred?" He shrugged his shoulders indifferently. "I remember my first, though. I married a horrid woman. She pushed me to my wits end, always wanting more, until I had nothing left to give. I sliced her open just to watch her squirm...Then, after I'd had my fun, I left her body in the gutter, so she might prove useful in feeding the vermin that dwelled there. It seemed a fitting end for a parasite." A sinister grin darkened his face. Madness seeped into his voice and twinkled in the pits of his eyes.

"You're crazy..." She spoke without considering the consequences.

"Oh? You don't believe me then?" he asked her, in a matter-of-fact tone.

She lay motionless. Her blood turned to ice in her

veins. She cursed herself for having spoken out in that moment.

"Would you like to see how I do it?" She noted a certain childlike excitement in his voice. "It's quite fascinating to watch, or so I've been told."

Without awaiting her response, he loosened his grip on the skillet, letting it clatter to the floor only inches from her head, before grabbing a handful of her hair. He started dragging her deeper into his lair. He passed through one of the innermost doors, with Catherine kicking and screaming at his heels.

"They've had countless names for me over the years," he rambled on, never showing any regard for her struggles. "Jack the Ripper, the Boogeyman, the Zodiac Killer." The list went on and on. Her insistent screams eclipsed his words, yet he never offered so much as a glance back over his shoulder. His attention seemed enveloped by those boastful proclamations.

Upon entering the kitchen, he let her drop unceremoniously to the linoleum floor. Catherine managed to roll onto her side, drinking in her new surroundings with cautious interest.

The kitchen seemed unremarkable. Not so much as a dish appeared out of place. Even the floor beneath glistened in the overhead light.

He left her there and moved to the kitchen table. Tracing his movements with her eyes, Catherine noticed a cardboard box sitting open on the table. Standing beside it, he turned his face toward her, grinning toothily as his hands dipped down into the box.

Even before the true spectacle began, Catherine noticed a strange light emanating from inside. The color appeared indistinct from where she lay, but it lit upon his features and seemed to grow increasingly brighter the closer his hands extended toward its source. Catherine never beheld the true form of the box's contents, but she had just enough time to ponder the possibilities.

As her captor's hands sunk out of view, a ripple trembled through the man's flesh, not unlike ripples on the surface of a pool of water. First, it worked its way up his arms. It caused the skin to contract in on itself before expanding once more. When it reached his face, the features there seemed to melt in on themselves. His clothes folded inwards, as the body beneath shrunk away, almost to nothing, before bulging outwards again, straining to contain the multiplied mass that rushed back into existence after its brief absence.

Catherine held her breath, watching the impossible unfold before her eyes. She forgot to exhale, keeping that single breath locked inside for the duration of his metamorphosis.

The man's legs compressed in on themselves, like a pair of mechanical stilts lowering to ground level. Either pantleg pooled around his feet, as his overall height lessened by at least three inches. She looked up in time to watch his hair retracting back into his scalp; it gradually brightened to a fiery reddish color and shaped itself in thin ringlets that curled out at uneven intervals.

He watched her through eyes left untouched by the passage of time. Their color stayed the same. The eyes were the only feature capable of revealing his true identity.

"What do you think?" he asked her, flashing a smile that reveled a new set of pearly whites. "Does it suit me?"

She watched the man they knew as Stewart Perkins transform before her eyes. It struck her speechless. She looked on, incapable of putting it all together in a way that made any logical sense.

After completing the change, he closed the flaps on the

cardboard box, sealing its contents within. He turned and started for her. His pantlegs, dragging on the floor now, concealed his bare feet. He stopped, standing over her, poised like a parent troubled by a particularly disobedient child. A frown creased the corners of his mouth.

"Do you understand now? I've changed like this more times than I could ever hope to count. Believe it or not, the alterations also extend beyond my physical appearance." He patted his stomach—now pudgier than in his former build. "It affects my entire anatomy, right down to the cellular level." He started pacing back and forth, becoming lost in his own words. "Even if I were to contract a life-threatening illness, I only need to change again to make myself as good as new. It's quite convenient really. Of course, I've always feared a heart attack might strike me down someday, but that hasn't happened yet."

"You're a monster." The words escaped her in a low hiss. Catherine no longer cared what became of her. She could never bear this knowledge and go on living a normal life. As far as she was concerned, her life had already ended the moment she realized the scope of his transgressions.

He knelt down beside her. Again, those never changing eyes seemed to perceive her inner workings. "I knew you were different even before we were formally introduced." His tone occupied a space between admiration and pity. Reaching for her, he brushed a strand of fallen hair from in front of her eyes. Catherine recoiled from his touch.

Anger shone through the mask of his face. Taking offense to her revulsion, his hand lunged forward. This time he grasped either side of her face. His clenched fingers formed dimples in the soft skin of her cheeks. She winced from the pain beginning to spread from where his fingers dug mercilessly into her jaw, but he forced her gaze to remain steadily upon him.

"I thought you had me this time. You had no idea, but I thought my luck had finally run out." He continued speaking in a calm manner that seemed untouched by his recent annoyance. "Then you just up and let me go. What utter fools you must have been!" He punctuated this last sentiment with an outburst of hearty laughter.

All the pieces were falling into place now. That final utterance of insult served as the straw that broke Catherine's will to persist. A cascade of emotion came boiling to the surface. Tears christened her cheeks, and a series of deep chested sobs racked her body from head to toe.

"Even so," he pressed onward, "I feared you might uncover the truth in the long run. I couldn't have that after only narrowly escaping with my freedom. You made it all too easy getting you here. I dropped the envelope on your desk myself, and no one so much as batted an eye…And why would they? I was already wearing a new face by then. Now, seeing how easy it was getting you to walk willingly into my trap, I wonder if my concerns were not misplaced."

His grip loosened. She lowered her head, turning her eyes away from him in disgust.

Her respite was short lived, however. He grabbed her by the hair once more and yanked until she felt herself being dragged across the kitchen. She twisted her neck sideways, trying to see where he was taking her, but his lumbering form obscured her view of what lay ahead. As her feet kicked out behind her, seeking purchase, and her body thrashed maddeningly, Catherine felt overcome by a distinct sense of powerlessness.

"So here we are at the end of your story," he went on, as if this were nothing more than a routine Sunday stroll. "Though, if it should come as any comfort, my story has only just begun." The thought of him going on like this for who knows how long sickened her more than the thought of her demise. "If God allows it, I will persevere until the end of time itself. God gave me this gift, after all, and only he can take it away from me. Until then, I will make the most of it." Insanity sprung forth through the cracks in his persona.

He shoved her head first into a dark and enclosed space. A heavy metal door swung shut behind her. She struggled back that way, but hardly had a chance to begin rationalizing any means of escape before the first burst of heat smacked her across the face. It spread and radiated over her body. The heat intensified over the passage of several painfully slow minutes.

The last thing Catherine Henson ever saw, as her clothes burned away, exposing the searing skin beneath, were those haunting, colorless eyes peering in at her. Sitting on the floor, face nearly pressed against the small, rectangular window in the door of the oven, he watched her final moments play out. Her writhing form brought him to the peak of mad pleasure. That overbearing emotion spewed forth in the form of shrill, high-pitched laughter; it seemed almost childlike in nature.

He bore the mentality of a destructive child, brandishing a hammer to bring ruin to one of his many toys, and for no reason other than to see what would happen. Somehow, seeing this toy shattered to pieces brought him more joy than its intended purpose. This child knew nothing of consequence. Basking in the short-lived pleasure that arose from indulging his animalistic nature, he drank it all in, until his soul turned as black as the flesh of a woman baked alive.

The Man in the Moon

Tabitha knelt before her bedroom window, with hands clasped, and deeply enthralled in the ritual of nightly prayer. Her parents taught her the importance of saying her prayers every night before bed. She embraced this notion with such fervor, that they no longer needed to remind her.

The full moon shone brightly in the starry night's sky outside her window. This bloated celestial body seemed to hang closer than normal. As adults, we know the moon could never draw nearer the Earth's surface, but in the mind of a child, the impossible remains ever present.

Through the girl's overexcited eyes, an infinite expanse of possibility lay beyond those twinkling stars and the great spherical monolith standing watch over the Earth's edge of the cosmos. Somewhere out there exists the basis for the god Tabitha's parents revered as the keystone of their existence. Tabitha wished she could behold the truth of that being, to give substance to the muddled image of their deity.

The young girl's eyes widened as moonlight lit upon her olive skin. For just the flicker of a moment, she thought she caught sight of the faintest hint of movement on the surface of that heavenly body. She thought she even recognized the bare outline of a man standing on its curved surface.

She squeezed her eyes shut with considerable effort, then opened them again, forcing her eyes to hone in on the site of the abnormality. Her eyes had not been playing tricks on her. There, upon the slope of the moon, stood the defined shape of a man cast in shadow.

Her eyes widened with awe. That sight shook her beliefs to their core. Everything the pastor preached at Sunday mass grew obsolete in comparison.

Clasping her hands together more tightly, she inclined them toward the moon. She prayed aloud just then, not afraid of being heard. She spoke the words and extended her devotion toward this newly discovered entity in the night's sky. She hoped her prayers would reach him.

Upon finishing, she blessed herself with the sign of the cross and crawled under the covers. With her cheek nestled into the welcome embrace of her pillow, Tabitha fell asleep. She dreamt only of the Man in the Moon. All the while she slept, moonbeams continued pouring in through her window, lighting her room in its dim afterglow.

Several uneventful hours passed before she woke to the sound of fluttering wings, like those of some overzealous bird taking to the sky. Rolling onto her side, she observed the silhouette of a man peering out through her now open window. He stood with his back to her.

With a hushed squeal of surprise, Tabitha sat bolt upright. A lens of fear clouded her better judgement, as she kept careful watch on her visitor.

"Quiet now, girl." He spoke in an echoing voice; it seemed to travel across some great distance. He never turned to look at her. "You need not be afraid, at least, I don't think you should have any reason." He sounded uncertain, and still on the verge of trying to piece together the finer details of their meeting.

She backpedaled slowly, until she felt the headboard pressed at her back. She stammered out her words, conveying an obvious disconnect between her brain and mouth. "A-Are...Are you him?" She finally managed to untangle her tongue.

He sounded slightly amused and on the verge of laughter. "Who is it you think I am?"

She found her voice more easily this time. "Are you God?" It sounded foolish even to her ears.

"God?" he asked, sounding perplexed. "I don't know that I understand this term. Is this 'God' a good person?"

Is God a good person? It seemed so strange to ponder the ethics of mankind's most divisive quandary. All the biblical stories of God's rage bearing down upon humanity, in the wake of their disobedience, argued against his purity, but there were also those tales of blessings bestowed upon those that welcomed his presence in their lives.

Tabitha simply could not arrive at an honest answer to his question. It overwhelmed her young mind and stayed her lips in solemn contemplation.

"I think maybe I understand..." His voice boomed throughout the room, reverberating off the walls and traveling back from all directions. "No, I'm not what you would call 'God.' At least, I don't think I am, but I am something greater than the foolish creatures inhabiting this rock." Although he belittled their kind, a touch of fondness lingered in his words.

"Do you know why I'm here?" he asked. His every word embodied a new riddle, laced with the mystery of the unknown.

She pulled the blanket up to her chin and shook her head. She felt much smaller all of a sudden, almost as if she were shrinking down to the size of a speck of dust in his presence.

Outside her window, the intensity of the moon's luminescence intensified. The man took a step forward, basking in its overhanging rays. His face remained cloaked in shadow, but the moon's light seemed to envelop him and flow through him.

"I think you'll understand later...Call upon me once more, when you've made your decision. I will come, and I will show you everything you desire. I alone hold the answers you seek." He left her with one final riddle before taking another step into the light. It swallowed him deeper in its embrace. His slender form dissipated before her very eyes. One minute, he was standing there (as clear as day), but in the next instant, the light shone through him, becoming something akin to a hologram of his true self.

Soon, he vanished altogether, with the light of the moon seeming to grow more somber.

He left Tabitha alone with her thoughts. She only half understood his proposition, playing right into the over-complicated nature of his plan. In his own enigmatic way, he left her on the cusp of thinking those wild thoughts, only fath-omable through a child's wayward imagination.

Tabitha slept that night and dreamt of the cosmos above. The wonders that dwell beyond the edge of their small pocket of existence fascinated her. Her dreams saw her em-barking on far-reaching adventures, where she made new friends in the strangest of places. A smile formed as she slum-bered, drifting deeper and deeper beneath the veil of sleep.

Given the chance, she already decided she would ask him to show her the stars. She wanted this more than any-thing.

She woke with these delusions still fresh in her brain. Deep down, the hope that these fantasies could become reality took root.

Rising from bed that morning, she glanced toward the window. Upon the windowsill sat a strange rock. An intricate array of honeycomb patters outlined its surface, and when she picked it up, it left a dark residue on her hands. Her new friend left this gift for her.

She hoped he would visit again that night, already de-termined to accept the terms of his offer—whatever they may be.

The very next night, she once more knelt beside her window, extending her clasped hands up toward the heavens, in hopes that her words would reach the Man in the Moon once more. His darkened outline stood in bold contrast against the luminous backdrop of the moon and the stars above; he seemed intermingled within the abyss that surrounded his saucer of inhabitance.

The moon shone a prominent shade of red that night, making her visitor seem all the more stoic, standing at the peak of its rocky surface. At first, he made no move from atop his perch.

She slid beneath the covers of her bed, much the same as the night before. Its silken embrace welcomed her, carrying her down into the liquid black of restless sleep. In her mind, she could hear the stars calling her name.

He waited for sleep to consume her before descending on wings unseen. Tabitha woke to the sound of movement beside her bed. She rolled over and peered through eyes still heavy with sleep. She found him sitting on the side of her bed, with his back still poised against her.

She sat up slowly. "Is it really you?" She seemed hesitant to accept his return.

Something seemed different about him that night. "Were you perhaps expecting God?" His tone harbored a slight edge of cynicism.

"I want to see the stars," she said at once, not wanting to consider his offer void.

"The stars?" He seemed to perk up at the mention. "I can show them to you, of course."

"Yes, please!" She already started moving closer, but an invisible force kept her from reaching him. "Can we go now?"

His head drooped slowly, severing his steady gaze up-on the splatter of starlight visible through her window. "If that's what you truly desire, then yes, we can." His tone grew dry and serious. To anyone other than a dream-bound child, that demeanor would have risen some suspicions, but Tabitha's curiosity never relented.

"It is! It's what I want more than anything!" Her excitement seemed all but tangible, springing forth from her every word.

"Well...Alright then..." His face started turning toward her for the first time. It appeared to take a sizable effort to pivot his body to look upon her, and by the time the light in the sky above lit upon his true form, Tabitha already regretted her decision.

Looking upon his face, it bore no resemblance to any-thing even remotely human. Instead, it bore a stone-like quali-ty, with sharp edges and deep, black craters etched into it, seeming to burrow down into the depths of his being. In fact, the indiscernible hulk, inhabiting the space where his face should have been, more closely resembled the moon rock she found waiting on her windowsill earlier that morning. Seeing it all now, without the mask of mystery to conceal the unbri-dled truth, Tabitha opened her mouth to scream.

As he saw the dread quivering in her eyes, he knew she would change her mind, but it was too late. She accepted his offer, and now he would claim her, as he claimed many before her.

Before her terrified scream could perforate the open air, a strong hand—rough and calloused—closed around her face. He moved with lightning speed, never allowing her the op-portunity to react. It gripped the sides of her face in a vice, pulling her up and onto her feet.

The light of the moon shone in through the window.

He pulled her toward the center of that ring of light. With the night sky at his back, he lifted her up off the floor. Her legs kicked and lunged out at him in mock defiance, like those of a lifeless ragdoll.

Soon, she became aware of a sound that resembled a vacuum's steady suction, but it only filled her ears for a brief moment, before it swallowed them both whole. He drew her into the void, allowing it to consume her, before leaving her lifeless body to drift through the depths of space.

Her desire carried her to the stars, and there she would remain, broken amidst the ruin of her innocence.

The Beast of Barony Road

Shortly after laying down to sleep for the night, his phone sounded its melodic jingle from where he left it charging on the bedside table. Flipping open the LED display, the indicator displayed a familiar number, with the word "Home" emblazoned above it.

"Hello?" He raised the device to his ear, speaking into it with a voice still groggy from his close proximity to sleep.

"Daddy?" The small voice on the other end sounded hushed and distant.

"Sweetie?" He recognized the voice of his daughter at once. "Shouldn't you be asleep?" He missed his daughter more than anything from that place he once called home.

"Daddy...I think something's wrong with mommy." She sounded frightened and on the brink of tears. "She's not acting right."

He suspected this strangeness centered around her addiction, but he could never disclose that secret to his daughter at such a young age. Seven-year-old Gloria may seem mature, but not so much so that she would prove capable of making heads or tails of his now ex-wife's alcoholism.

"Strange how, sweetie?" he pressed her for more information.

Presently, Theodore Glenn finds himself locked in a battle for custody of his daughter, with her mother, Beverly, fighting him at every turn. Perhaps, Beverly would actually go over the deep end this time, and that would give him a real fighting chance of getting Gloria back in his care.

"She's breaking everything, daddy. She has all our stuff in a big pile on the floor." Gloria seemed appalled by this.

He shook his head solemnly; a shadow of worry filled the lines that formed there.

"Daddy, I'm scared..." The slight tremor in her voice sent Theodore's temper roaring into full-blown rage.

"Don't worry, sweetie. Daddy's on his way." He disconnected the call and sat up slowly. The deadened phone slipped from unsteady fingers. His bones seemed to creak beneath the surface, as he swung his feet over the edge of the mattress. A dull ache throbbed in the joints of his legs. At this rate, exhaustion would overtake him soon, but first, he needed to make sure Gloria was out of harm's way.

He dressed in a hurry. His truck—its surface faded from deep black to a shade of washed-out gray from regular use over the past six years—waited in the motel's dimly lit parking lot. As he climbed behind the wheel, he cursed Beverly's name under his breath.

This needed to be the last straw to shift the favor of the court in his direction. Gloria would only suffer more if he allowed her to live out the rest of her childhood under Beverly's temperamental gaze. Gloria deserved better than that. They owed her a normal childhood.

He set off down that long, deserted stretch of Barony Road. The digital readout on the dashboard recorded the time at 1:42AM. He left in a hurry, failing to take the time to consider the bigger picture. As he drove headlong toward what he considered a valiant rescue attempt, his cellphone lay forgotten amidst a sprawl of bedding.

Barony Road formed a bridge between the small town of Shawnee and the rest of the world beyond. The venture saw him passing through a corridor of tightly encroaching forestry on all sides. Tall trees and high grass rose up from every direction. In those small hours of night, the woods seemed even more monstrously vast and mysterious. The thought of venturing forth into that darkness would drive even the most battle-hardened individuals into a fit of panic.

To Theodore's misfortune, nine miles down the road from the welcoming glow of the motel's "Vacancy" sign (and still twelve miles outside the Shawnee town limits) his truck's engine began to sputter, sending thick, black smoke signals into the starry sky above. A series of warning lights flashed before his eyes, and the truck crawled to a stop on the soft shoulder of the road.

He took these new frustrations out on the steering wheel, pounding his fists down over and over, until a dull pain reverberated back through his aching body. He cranked the ignition over and over, praying the engine would catch and roar back to life. Instead, it whimpered and whined down to dead silence once more.

Only then did he awaken to the absence of his cell phone. This cruel turn-of-events found him stranded and cut off from all civilization. He could only hope some wayward soul would pass in time, but by then, he would surely lose the upper hand he hoped to gain from finding Beverly awash in a drunken stupor. If he ever hoped to snatch his daughter back out of her grasp, he needed to capitalize on her faults.

Climbing down from the cab of his truck, taking a breath of crisp autumn air, he found his senses overly attuned to even the subtle sound of rustling leaves and the chirrup of crickets at play amidst the high grass. He stood for a moment on hardpan asphalt, considering his isolation through eyes darting in all directions.

The sense of being watched gnawed at him. The hairs on the nape of his neck stood at attention. He almost found himself retreating into the safety of his truck, nearly opting to abandon his venture, before a sense of obligation stilled his feet.

He turned to look both ways down the long stretch of road. He hoped to glimpse some sign of life approaching from either direction, but his prayers were quickly dashed by the darkness encroaching at every turn. Alone, with only the faint whisper of wind billowing through innumerable treetops, he found himself utterly alone and with no means of salvation.

A sound caught his ear just then. He jerked his head toward a rustling in the underbrush nearby. Listening intently, he failed to pinpoint the exact source of the disturbance.

Darkened shapes loomed like towers. He spun himself in circles, growing dizzy from his frantic search, and still, that murmur amidst the depths of the forest—deep and menacing in nature—crept closer still.

There, on the boundary of the world ruled by man, where nature still held dominance, Theodore found himself coming face to face with a terror beyond his wildest imaginings.

The Beast of Barony Road had long been an urban legend of sorts, often exchanged over the dying embers of a campfire in the hours when nightmares took shape. With no solid proof to back the countless claims of the Beast's existence, they were more often chalked up as nothing more than the common bear or mountain cat sighting, but no one really seemed to know for sure.

Until now…

Theodore, frozen in fear, watched as the behemoth stepped forth through the dense underbrush. The forest itself seemed to quiver and distance itself from the Beast, as if wishing to rid itself of the creature's indomitable presence. Standing on four legs, it lumbered at a height of over eight-feet. Its bristling fur appeared thickly matted with dirt and other debris reminiscent of its natural habitat. Bright red eyes peered out from its broad, flat face, seeming locked upon Theodore's position. Those were only his initial observations before deciding to make a run for it.

Gloria's face swam to the surface of his mind, as his survival instincts kicked into high gear. He barely made it more than six feet down the road from where his truck came to rest, before the Beast took off after him. It took but one leaping stride of the creature's oversized legs to catch its wary prey mid-flight.

The Beast's fangs proved sharper than any blade, and they ended Theodore's struggles with a single, gnashing chomp. They tore his body clean in two, leaving the two halves connected only by a gory tangle of entrails, stretched taunt at either end. The scream that bubbled inside the man's throat never reached open air. Instead, he died choking on a heavy torrent of blood. It filled his airways, and darkness rose to meet him. The Beast heaved the two halves of his lifeless body up and into its great maw, leaving nothing but a thin puddle of blood to mark Theodore Glenn's passing.

Local law enforcement would discover his truck abandoned on the side of the road, and the blood splatter nearby called forth a search party to comb the woods adjacent. They never found any sign of Theodore's remains, but the Beast's colossal tracks were discovered leading away from the scene.

This story would come to live in infamy, further solidifying the legend of the Beast of Barony Road for generations to come.

Azure Flags

An array of royal blue flags lined the stone peaks of the cobbled towers of that fabled northern kingdom. Once lost to time itself, it became something akin to legend.

The annals of history ignored its possible existence, while government officials openly reject the very notion. Yet the tales spun on and on, alluding to some truth behind this lost utopia. Most regard this nameless kingdom as not but fiction, while others live to question the mystery of the unknown.

Carefully navigating the frozen wilderness at the edge of civilization, a lonely silver pickup truck rolls to a stop on the frost encrusted shoulder of a dead-end road. They reached the end of the line—in a literal sense—with no sign of any manmade dwelling as far as the eye could see.

Four snowsuit-clad figures clamored out from within the truck's cramped interior. They were each dressed in layer upon layer of clothing to defend their fragile bodies against the harsh northern climates. Tightly woven masks adorned the lower half of their face, with their eyes encased behind pairs of thick goggles.

The masks muffled their speech to a degree, while the roaring wind further deafened them, but huddled close together, they were still able to cement the plans for the next stage of their endeavor. "Your supposed lost kingdom is still some ways off from here, or at least that seems to be the general consensus." The man amplified his voice to be heard over the insistent churning of the elements. He raised one gloved hand in the direction of a thick cluster of snow-covered evergreens. "This is as far as the road can take us. We'll have to go on foot from here."

"Are you sure about this?" A voice rose beside him, belonging to a petite woman hidden beneath her burdensome attire.

"It's not too late to turn back, Sue." A third figure shouldered up to her. This man (built like an ox) bore the added weight of a hefty pack, containing an assortment of supplies deemed necessary to their survival.

She simply shook her head dismissively. "No, we've already come too far to turn back."

Their final member stayed by the open passenger side door of the truck. A backpack stood open on the seat, and this fourth snowsuit-clad figure rummaged through its contents, desperate to locate something of importance. "Where did I put it?" she exclaimed in a shrill embodiment of panic. "I know I brought it!"

"Looking for something?" Their self-appointed leader appeared at her back and effortlessly produced her lost possession from one of the oversized pockets in his jacket. He held it up for her to see, only to have it snatched away from him.

"What did I tell you about touching my stuff, Jack?" The words escaped her mouth in a hiss of annoyance, but there was no denying the relief she felt at having it back.

She clutched the object close to her chest. It was a small, hardcover book with a simplistic drawing of a stereotypical king, queen, and princess etched upon the cover, and the silhouette of a castle loomed in the background. That curious book, titled "The Azure Keep," once belonged to her father. It was given to her as a gift on her tenth birthday, accompanied by her father's recount of the tradition that saw the book passing from generation to generation.

"Why did you bring that stupid thing along anyway?" Jack remarked without restraint. "Does Jenny need me to read her a bedtime story?" He tore into bales of laughter that only abated when her outstretched hand struck his safely cushioned chest.

"You need to cut the shit. This is serious." Jennifer saw little humor in the matter. "If you can't take this seriously, you should just wait here." She relinquished her hold on the book, stowing it safely in the front of her jacket.

"And what? Freeze to death, while you guys get yourselves lost in the woods? No thanks! You know you need me to keep you from getting into trouble." That same egocentric attitude once helped Jack score with every cheerleader at North Harding High School in the prime of his adolescence. Some individuals just never seemed to emerge from the shell of their youth.

The larger of the two men cleared his throat impatiently. "If you haven't noticed, we're freezing our asses off over here, so if you could save trying to get into each other's pants for another time, that'd be great." Rodey showed little emotion, aside from the occasional annoyance at what he considered "childish squabbling."

"He's right. If we lose the light of day, we might as well turn back now." Susan, meek and distanced from their chummy gathering, far exceeded the intellect of the others by leaps and bounds. She knew their chances were fleeting at best.

Together these four formed an unlikely alliance. Jennifer Quinton, Jack Harlow, Susan Addison, and Rodey Simmons set forth into the wilderness at the world's northernmost reach.

As it happened, the wilderness proved to be the least of their worries.

Earlier that day, at the crack of dawn, they started their drive north from a sleepy lodge town, where they spent the night prior. The sun touched its highest point at the start of their hike into uncharted territory. Upon discovering a clearing at the heart of the woods, the sun's arch neared the opposite horizon.

"How can this be..." Jennifer's eyes widened behind protective lenses.

That expanse seemed untouched by the forces of nature, while barren wilderness encircled at every turn. It appeared picturesque and awash in its own splendid beauty.

In fact, the stillness of their new surroundings seemed somehow unnatural. A frigid wind cut between even the thickest brambles of the surrounding wooded area, but its power held no claim over this timeless retreat. The frostbitten husks at their back continued to sway listlessly in whatever direction Mother Nature deemed fit, but not so much as a draft reached them at the edge of the clearing.

Jennifer stepped forward on legs that felt unsteady. "I must be dreaming...And here I'd been sure this would all be for nothing."

Several feet from where they emerged, a cobbled road—of the likes no modern vehicle had ever traversed—wound its way up a mild embankment to the arched gate of a castle that appeared unchanged over the years. Seeing the castle gave substance to the long-overlooked rumors. The encompassing stone walls displayed a unique bluish tint, further emphasized by the color of the banners draped from the highest battlements. A matching set of flags lay motionless at the top of the spires that marked each corner of the castle's perimeter. Both the flags and the banners bore a crescent moon insignia, which also appeared at regular intervals throughout Jennifer's childhood keepsake.

"What? You mean you didn't actually think we'd find anything out here? And still, you dragged us all this way?" Jack lashed out at Jennifer with a hint of defiance.

Jack and Jennifer descended into a heated back and forth. The others paid them little mind.

At the same time, Susan reached out and touched Rodey's arm, almost trying to convey her feelings through physical contact. "Something feels wrong about this place," she told him in a hushed tone, intending the words for his ears only.

"I know…" Rodey agreed with her. "I feel it too." Even his voice bore a certain resentful edge. "It feels like a grave-yard."

Two months before embarking on the expedition that would ultimately prove life-changing, the four would-be adventurers gathered around a table in the library of their shared university.

The once high school playboy, who from an early age learned to pluck the heartstrings of every girl that crossed his path, still wore the face of boyhood. His features were handsome in their own right, but they still exhibited the soft angles of youth. Of course, he would use this to his advantage, adding it to his arsenal of dastardly tricks.

Jennifer was tall by most accounts, with shoulder-length brunette hair that half screened her pale face. She glowered at Jack from across the table. Her brown eyes were like that of a hawk set upon its prey. "I knew I should have never included you. You're still the same ignorant asshole you were in high school."

"Whoa now!" Jack broke her tangent in an attempt at self-defense. The grin that accompanied his protest told another story altogether. "I'll try playing nice as long as you don't go blowing a gasket at every little thing I say. Deal?" He ran one hand through his short black hair. His charisma often carried him through even the most oppressive situations, but Jennifer remained impervious to his silver tongue.

Jennifer heaved a sigh in open defeat. "Fine. Do what you want." Then, under her breath: "You always do."

Jack flashed a triumphant, half-cocked smile in her direction.

Having known Jack since their early elementary years, Jennifer developed an immunity that protected her from his charms. She perceived a pit of snakes writhing beneath the surface of his false face, and she never allowed herself to forget all the broken hearts he left in his wake.

"What's this all about anyway?" Rodey made no attempt to hide his impatience. His eyes narrowed to thin slits. The dark complexion of his face masked a bubbling tidal wave of emotion.

Susan eyed Jennifer knowingly from where she sat close at Rodey's side. Already having a good idea what this was all about, she felt apprehensive. Sitting next to Rodey made the five-foot-nothing girl appear even more childlike in comparison. Susan's natural blonde hair clung to the sides of her face, forming thin ringlets where it came to rest.

From beneath the table, Jennifer produced the book she would later carry to the edge of civilization. She positioned it at the middle of the table, where all in attendance could plainly see. "This is why I called you all here today," she told them, holding her breath and waiting for the outburst she knew would come.

"You called us here to talk about a book?" Rodey spoke in disbelief.

Susan only nodded her head slowly. Having been friends with Jennifer for some time, that book and its contents were nothing new to her.

"I'm sure you've all heard what I'm about to tell you in

passing. It's a well-known story, even if most regard it as a fairy tale of sorts, but I have reason to believe there's more to it than that." Jennifer half expected they might write her off as crazy, yet a part of her hoped they would at least stay long enough to humor her.

"And what makes you think that?" Jack's response bore no ill-intent, but it lacked any genuine consideration.

"My father used to travel the country lecturing on cultural mythology," Jennifer dove headfirst into the chain of events leading up to this meeting. "Modern myths, often called urban legends, fascinated him. Most, he admitted, were nothing more than baseless nonsense, but some bore striking correlations to real and often unexplained events." She inclined her head toward the book at the center of the table. "This story called to him like no other. In his notes, he even speculated its most probable whereabouts. He died before he could set about proving his hypothesis. I just want to see his life's work completed." She left out the part where her father had become a laughingstock among his peers, instead choosing to paint him as a potential genius.

Each attendee harbored their own touch of skepticism, choosing to listen all the same. There would be time for dispute and rebuttal later, but first they needed to garner a better understanding of her motives.

"The tale of 'The Azure Keep' goes as follows..." Jennifer set about recapping the story contained within those pages. "Once upon a time, there existed a kingdom blessed with unrivaled peace and prosperity. One evening, the benevolent Azure King extended an invitation to all the people of the land, calling for joyous celebration on the eve of a truce between their flourishing kingdom and the forest realm to the south. To further strengthen the alliance, the king's own daughter was slated to marry the heir of that less bountiful nation.

"The unique architectural qualities of the Azure Keep were long regarded as somehow mystical, with some even associating the kingdom's splendid growth with some invisible force contained within the castle's walls. The stone used in its construction shone with a hint of blue, unlike anything seen elsewhere in that time. More distinct still, as night fell over the Azure Keep, these unique building blocks projected an eerie, almost ghostly aura. There were some that even believed the founder of the Keep struck a deal with the gods to ensure the success of their kingdom.

"As you might suspect, many of the neighboring regions grew envious of their wealth and wished to see them struck asunder. You'd think that would garner mistrust in the subjects of the king who presided over the Azure Keep, but instead, they sought to better the world around them.

"That brings us to the eve of the wedding. The Azure King hoped that by performing the sacred ritual there, in the heart of the Keep, they might quell any further conflict between them and their restless neighbor.

"Unfortunately for those seeking peace, a terrible tragedy befell the Azure Keep that very night. Before the betrothed could exchange their everlasting vows, a stranger, cloaked all in black, intruded upon the joyous occasion, seeking an audience with the Azure King. He promised a wonderous gift befitting of the occasion.

"That gift, concealed within a drawstring satchel, appeared from a fold in the stranger's garb. He carefully laid this untold bounty at the Azure King's feet. The king collected the offering and proceeded to free it from its encasement. Once out in the open, a brilliant beam of blue light spread throughout the hall. That radiance shone from the center of a perfectly rounded gemstone, as it lay upon the lap of that kingdom's eternal ruler.

"None present ever beheld the full beauty of that treasure. The light's intensity grew and overtook the castle, and those attending that merry occasion found themselves drifting into an endless slumber. Some say, that even to this day, somewhere beyond the understanding of modern society, the people of those two nations continue to sleep the years away, preserved in a supernatural state of hibernation, defying the laws of time itself..."

Jennifer allowed the silence that followed to run its course.

They entered the Azure Keep through a high arching gateway. An expansive entryway, done up in ornate shades of gold and silver, loomed around the four young explorers. They could do nothing to contain their honest amazement.

"This cannot be real..." Jennifer found herself in a state of heightened disbelief, exceeding even that of her traveling companions.

A towering stairwell ascended to another monstrous door situated atop a large stone landing. It called to them, promising yet unseen mysteries beyond. They mounted the stairs one at a time. Each step permeated the soundless atmosphere of that forgotten place.

Jennifer felt her lips twisting into a smile. For her, a smile in itself was a rare sight to behold, and all at once, the shadows that lingered in the lines of her face retreated back into obscurity.

Meanwhile, a seed of doubt took root in Susan's gut, growing more prominent the nearer they drew to that door. She immediately recognized a strong weight growing atop her shoulders. She looked to Rodey for reassurance, hoping to see his equally troubled expression reflected back at her, but he seemed only focused on their surroundings. To ease her troubled mind, she reached out and grasped Rodey's much larger hand; he returned the sentiment, squeezing her hand reassureingly. Their relationship had no need for spoken acknowledgement, each serving as a pillar of support for the other.

They were halfway to the top now. Jennifer showed no sign of stopping. She pulled ahead of the pack. Even if she were to recognize the looming danger in the air, she would never allow herself to turn back.

Reaching the door at the top of the stairs, Jennifer threw her weight against it. The door stood at least ten feet tall, but it slid inwards with ease. As the gap between door and frame grew, a thin stream of light escaped, painting their cloaked faces in its blue glow.

A large gathering hall lay beyond. Rows of tables lined the interior, and there, slumped in their seats, were the littered bodies of those slumbering partygoers. At the head of the room, situated atop a raised platform, stood the thrones of the two royal families.

"My god..." Susan gasped and squeezed her beloved's hand more tightly. She recognized the source of that supernatural light at once, nestled on the lap of the Azure King.

"Yes...It is real." Jennifer breathed the words through clenched teeth. Her smile widened. She touched the rectangular bulge in her jacket.

The heavy air grew increasingly burdensome to Susan. As the calming light filled her eyes, a haze formed there. When the weight became too much for her to bear, she lost her footing and tumbled sideways. Rodey quickly dropped to one knee in an attempt to catch Susan midfall, but instead, he too fell victim to that long-forgotten spell. He came to rest upon the cold, stone floor at Susan's side. Each breathed slowly, lost to a timeless slumber.

Jack stood frozen. "What's going on?" He looked from Susan to Rodey, clearly disturbed by this sudden turn of events. "What's wrong with them?"

Jennifer, on the other hand, never so much as offered a glance in their direction. Her eyes remained front-facing. She stepped forward, unwilling to turn her gaze from the prize at hand.

"Jen?" Jack called to her from where his feet stayed glued. "Don't you think we'd better get out of here?"

No response. Her footsteps echoed in rhythm with the fluctuating pulse of that cursed artifact.

"I think we'd better go get help." Jack knelt beside their fallen friends. He became the voice of reason amidst Jennifer's blinding obsession. Hoping to at least save himself, he turned to descend back to the safety of the outside world. He managed only a single step forward. Collapsing at the top of the stairs, he became just another piece of the backdrop.

A maddening desire overwrote Jennifer's better judgement. With eyes bulging, she stood at the foot of the Azure King's throne. She reached one trembling hand forward, seeking to take hold of that unfathomable power.

The grizzled ruler of the Keep slept with his crown slightly askew atop his head. As Jennifer's grasp neared the king's last worldly possession, his recently lifeless hand leapt forward, encircling Jennifer's wrist and tightening there. She could feel her bones creaking within that ironclad manacle.

"NO!" The words exploded from the mouth of the Azure King. "YOUR PRESENCE IS UNWELCOME HERE!"

Jennifer fought desperately to pull her hand free from his grip. The magic of the sphere (so close now) threatened to overwhelm even her.

"YOU KNOW NOT WHAT YOU HAVE DONE!"

The king's eyes opened wide and rolled back to reveal only white.

"Let go of me!" Jennifer shrieked and clawed at the king's hand. "I've come too far to let you stop me now."

An electric current passed between Jennifer and the king. A series of images filled her mind. They were his sub-conscious memories brought to life.

(*The stranger knelt at the foot of the throne. He wore the tattered remains of a black cloak, while bloodstained bandages concealed the entirety of his face.*)

Jennifer found herself dropping to her knees, as unspoken knowledge flowed through her.

(*"I have come with an urgent message, mi'lord…In my possession, I hold a weapon capable of silencing the lives of all who call these lands their home."*)

Jennifer's face contorted in an agonized grimace. That voice from the past made her head throb, and a fresh stream of blood descended from either nostril.

(*"Mi'lord, I have come seeking your aid. This power needs to be hidden where no enemy will ever reach it…"*)

Feeling torn asunder, half of Jennifer's mind occupied her own body, while the other half drifted back into the past. She became two unique individuals, each occupying different points in the timeline of that fabled place.

(*The stranger produced a drawstring bag fashioned from some otherworldly material. He held it up for the king to see.*)

The remnant of that bag lay at the king's feet even now, forgotten in the face of the treasure contained within.

"*YOU HAVE BROUGHT THE DARKNESS WITH YOU!*" Again, that voice from within of the once peace-loving king's mouth. It brought dire accusations to Jennifer and her accomplices.

The link between past and present severed, snapping

Jennifer back into herself. She struggled to maintain a hold of her conscious awareness long enough to make sense of this newly acquired knowledge.

A great many truths lingered in the king's curt tone.

A darkness lingered in the pit of Jennifer's heart, and that same malice sought release now. She squeezed her eyes shut, only to feel a pressure building there. Upon concentrateing, she recognized the talons of some foreign monstrosity trying to claw its way out from inside her mind. That formless creature sought to acquire that most formidable of magical weapons.

The king's grip tightened on her wrist. *"YOU BROU-GHT THEM TO OUR DOORSTEP!"*

"No! No! No!" Jennifer denied the fact, unwilling to admit that she allowed herself to become the vessel for some dark force.

"NOW YOU WILL SLEEP HERE WITH US FOREVER!"

Sleep overtook her, dragging her down into the depths of its everlasting embrace. She would join the others there, as listless protectors of a power they never fully understood.

The unique construct of the Azure Keep served as a prison of sorts, containing that power within its walls. Should their defenses fail, the entirety of the world would bask in the light of tranquility, ending all strife in one fell swoop.

As Jennifer's plight drew to a close, the door to the gathering hall swung closed of its own accord. With no one left to hear the clatter it made in sealing itself against the threat of the outside world, only silence remained to accompany its undisturbed inhabitants.

Eventually, the time would come for another foolhardy adventurer to set forth in hopes of unraveling its mysteries, but they too would fall victim to their own curiosity.

Two Halves

"Do you still remember the day we first met?" she asked him, already convinced of his response.

"Wasn't it in Mrs. Abadad's eighth grade math class?" He sounded indecisive and unconvinced by his own answer.

She was already shaking her head. "No, it was a couple years before that, at a birthday party. We were only kids, but you spent most of the day pulling on my pigtails and calling me names. They were only the kinds of dumb insults grade schoolers sling back and forth at one another from across the playground, but I still remember bursting into tears and telling my mom what you'd done."

"Oh...That's embarrassing." Her accusation caught him unaware. He bore no recollection of those events. "I don't think you'd ever told me that before."

"We were just dumb kids back then, Greg. I didn't think it really mattered."

"It must have mattered if you still remember after all these years."

His words rang true, but still she refused him open admittance. "Do you even remember how long it's been?"

"How long?" He needed no time in thinking this one through. "It's been just over twenty years since our *separation*." That last word lingered on his tongue, seeming almost exaggerated.

"Our separation?" She immediately latched onto his flawed recollection of their breakup. "Is that what you've taken to calling it?"

He shrugged his shoulders dismissively and slouched back as far as the seat would allow. "What would you call it?"

Her face reddened, as the memory bubbled to the surface. "What would I call it?" Her tone mocked his aversion, while maintaining a cool disposition. "I think calling it a betrayal of trust is a fair assessment, but if you really want to get right down to it, I'd say you broke my heart."

"Like you said, Sarah, we were just dumb kids. We didn't yet know where our lives were taking us."

That seemed to touch a nerve. "We were just kids? Jesus, Greg, we were going on thirty when I caught you sneaking around behind my back."

He made no attempt to deny it. "At least I had the dumb part right."

"You were pretty dumb..." The intensity in the air seemed to dissipate some.

"Still, it didn't take you very long to get over me. You were already jumping in the sack with my best friend only a month later." Even as his mouth formed the words, he knew presenting them in such a blatant manner would prove disastrous in the long run.

"I never once cheating on you...Richard was there for me after you'd left me broken and alone." A cold fire burned within her eyes.

"I'm just saying, I don't feel I deserve to be blamed for the entirety of what happened between us." He felt backed into a corner.

"If you've been holding a grudge against Richard all this time, then why are you even here?" She held nothing back.

"I don't hold it against him..." He looked down. His hands were resting in his lap; they felt distant and powerless to act under the circumstances. "He's the only friend I've managed to keep over the years."

"Then just try to be supportive for once in your life. Your friend is in there, life hanging by a thread, and all you can think to do is accuse me of something you know never happened."

He wanted to further insinuate how she opened the

door to this discussion, only to quickly reconsider and steer the conversation into safer waters. "How did it happen anyway?"

She turned back the clock. Face growing pale, she found herself reliving every troubling detail through her mind's eye. "We were just sitting down to dinner when he started complaining of pains in his chest. I can still see the way his mouth kept on opening and closing, just before he keeled over. It was horrible."

He trembled at the thought of his oldest friend succumbing to that silent killer—the stealthiest of assassins. "What have the doctor's been saying?"

"Not a whole lot. They brought him here in the ambulance and told me they were going to have to operate right away. I called you right after that. That's all I've heard so far." She left out the part where the thought of sitting alone in that dimly lit waiting room, unsure if her husband would live or die, frightened her nearly as much as the ordeal itself.

"I'm sure he'll be fine. He's a fighter. You know that better than anyone." He said this as a way of pushing back his own disquieting thoughts.

"I know…If not for Richard's unmoving determination, our marriage probably would have failed a long time ago."

"Right, so you have nothing to worry about." He hoped he sounded convincing.

"Did he ever tell you about the miscarriage?"

He shook his head, still not looking her in the eye. "No… It's not exactly the sort of thing you'd talk about over beer and football."

"It happened two years into our marriage." Reminiscing made it easier to escape the present. It let some of the pent-up steam trickle out into the atmosphere. "After months of trying, the pregnancy test came back positive. We were so excited. You can't even imagine."

He thought he heard the ghost of that excitement in her voice now. "The two of you would have made excellent parents." He could think of nothing else to say in the extended silence that followed.

"Not long into the pregnancy, I kept feeling like something was wrong. Then came the blood, all but proving my suspicions. Richard rushed me to the emergency room in a panic. They ran a lot of tests, but it was already too late. Our fantasy life came to a screeching halt."

He mulled it over, wondering how he might have reacted in that situation. "And there weren't any signs before?"

She shook her head. "No, like I said, I had a gut feeling that something was wrong, but never anything concrete."

"And you and Richard never thought to try again?"

Now she turned her eyes away in turn. "I wasn't myself for a while after that. I retreated back into myself. Richard was always so gung-ho about having kids, but I think he saw what it did to me and never mentioned it again. He did that for me."

"What about you? Didn't you want to start a family?" He shared a bed with her once, many years before, but she never showcased such severe emotional turmoil in his presence.

"Not after what happened. Looking back on things now, we maybe could have done things differently, but I don't regret that choice. We found true happiness together."

A faint smile touched the corner of his mouth. "That's all that matters, right?" He envied what they shared together and yearned for something similar. Yet somehow, he knew it would always linger just out of reach for him.

"What about you, Greg? Whatever happened to the woman you left me for?"

The truth came as little surprise. "Oh, not much. As it happened, I was only one of countless suitors she had lined up to share her bed. The truth came out eventually, and when it did, I ended up drawing the short straw."

Reality often caught up to those that justified unfaithfulness. "Now you know how I felt?"

"I do…" A sharp pang of guilt struck him suddenly. "It's not a pleasant feeling."

His remorse seemed to start the process of mending the rift between them. "You traveled for some time, didn't you?" She never bothered to commit the finer details of his life to memory. "You never found love again?"

"Sure, I found love on several occasions, or at least I thought it was love. There's a difference between falling in love just for the sake of falling in love and falling in love because you actually want to spend your life with that person. I just never found the real thing."

"I'm sorry to hear that…" The sentiment reflected her genuine intent.

"It's probably a good thing we didn't work out. You were better off with Richard in the long run," he admitted, partly to himself.

"I think you're probably right." She saw no reason to sugarcoat her response. Their relationship seemed doomed to fail from day one. His self-serving tendencies stood in bold contrast to Richard, who never asked for anything in exchange for his love and devotion.

He laughed suddenly. The sudden exuberance seemed unnatural in this setting. "I guess it's about time we agreed on something."

"Don't take it personally." She turned to him and really looked at him for the first time in as long as she could remember. "I've always been a hard person to love."

"Ditto," he remarked, never hesitating. "I think I probably still am."

Shaking her head, she actually felt herself beginning to smile. "No, I wouldn't say that. You have a way of growing on people. You're not like me. I came from a broken home. My father used to beat my mother for sport, and when he grew tired of hearing her scream and beg, he would turn the belt on me."

A cold silence settled over the room. Her most private confession hung between them.

She broke the silence herself. "I came into adulthood without ever knowing what it meant to be loved. It made it hard for me to ever return the sentiment. Richard changed that for me."

"Yeah...You have me beat there..." He stepped carefully, considering the impact of his words. "My parents were constantly showering me with affection and praise. I'm not sure where I went wrong."

"There's nothing wrong with you," she pressed the fact. "You're just different is all."

"If you say so..." A shadow descended over him. A fresh vein of self-loathing and regret opened just beneath the surface. He felt every ounce of pain he ever inflicted on her writhing to the surface.

In the end, she found a life with Richard, which made it difficult for her to see things from his perspective. Just as she opened her mouth in retort, the double doors at the far end of the waiting room swung open. Richard's doctor stepped forth.

They both held their breath, hoping for good news.

Seven

June 7th, 2017

I've decided to keep a record of everything, mainly as a means of justifying the truth of the matter, but also for the sake of my sanity. If you should happen to be reading this, just know that I'm not crazy by any means. I wish I could say I were making this all up, but everything that's happened to me over this last year has been all too real.

I used to live what some might call a normal life. I was married, working a nine-to-five job as a custodian at the local high school, and we were as happy as any other middle-class American family in this day and age.

That all changed after the accident. I lost my wife on July 7th, 2016. It's taken almost a full year for me to decide to share my experiences.

Remember the date. It's going to be important, I promise.

It really was just an accident. I know what you're probably already thinking, but I in no way contributed to the death of my wife.

Her passing led to a life of solitude for me. Shut off from the world, I mourned and tried to forget the pain that hid behind every facet of the homestead. Photographs of our happiest moments tore deep into the fabric of my being, and eventually I decided to cast those talismans that bore the most prominent memories into the hearth, with a monstrous fire set to burn even the ghosts that dwelled within.

I know you're waiting for me to go into more detail on the accident, but I don't feel like talking about it just yet. It hurts too much to even think about, let alone put those thoughts down on paper. It was only an accident, and that's all I'm going to say.

As for the date, you might even say it's the most vital

piece of information I've disclosed thus far. It holds a certain candle of clarity to something I've long suspected since my years of boyhood.

Seven is a powerful and deadly number that holds dominion over my life. I was seven-years-old when my mother passed away. Seven years later, my father decided to take a premature leave of absence from my life. I found myself in the care of my aunt and uncle, who just so happened to live at 77 Kneble Lane. I graduated from high school in 1997, and I met the woman I would one day marry later that same year. Seven years after we met, we exchanged vows in a rickety chapel, nestled at the intersection of Main and Seventh Street.

Of course, we didn't know it then, but 1997 was the year this all really started. None of this would have happened if not for our meeting.

It's more than a little bit scary just considering all the coincidental connections interwoven throughout my lifetime, but once you start putting the clues together, allowing the bigger picture to take shape, it becomes absolutely terrifying. Looking at it now, I've come to believe my life holds some grander significance. Those signs were the workings of the universe, although I often tried to play them off as nothing more than sheer happenstance. I see the light now, and there's no going back after glimpsing the dark lining behind the whole of reality.

Even the date of my wife's death played into that notion.

I used to try to ignore all the signs, but I can no longer turn a blind eye to what lies hidden around every corner. I've seen the fingers of darkness close at hand, and I know they orchestrated her passing, just as that same puppeteer connected the dots that drew us together in love.

I'm sorry. I can't keep getting ahead of myself like this.

There's still a lot to tell before I reveal the truth of the matter. I'll get there in time, but please bear with me for now.

I need to get back to the importance of that number.

Seven days after my wife's funeral, with the memory of an empty casket descending into her earthly tomb, I saw her again. Slinking out from the shadowy corner of the bedroom we once shared, my beloved came back for me. It would seem even death couldn't keep us apart.

Her face was still gone. I could see boney patches showing through the gristle of what little flesh and muscle remained. She peered at me through empty sockets. Even in that state, I could never mistake the beauty that once drew me into blissful enchantment. We were bound by that formidable number and the forces at work behind it.

We're going on a year from that day, and only now have I begun to realize the importance of everything. That's why I decided to start writing it all down. It needs to be told.

It's getting late, and I've already written a lot. She'll be coming soon. She always does. I need to prepare.

If I've forgotten anything important, I'll write about it tomorrow. For now, I need to go.

I need to talk to her. I need to be with her. I need her to know that it was only an accident.

June 9th, 2017

I forgot to write yesterday. I ended up sleeping for most of the day. That's become the norm for me. I sleep all day and spend my nights with her.

I think I'm starting to forget things, and they're things that used to be important to me. At least they seemed important at the time.

Now, I think I know what's truly important.

If I could remember everything I'd forgotten, I'd make a list here, but I think I've even begun to forget just what it is I've forgotten. I'm not sure that even makes sense, but it did in my head, and that's all that matters.

That's just how forgetting works.

I'm not feeling well all of a sudden. Maybe I'd best put off writing the rest until tomorrow. I can't bring myself to find the right words.

She'll be coming soon, anyway. I need to be ready when she does.

Please just remember that one thing I told you in the beginning: I am NOT crazy.

June 10th, 2017

I think I'm finally ready now. I have to tell the rest.

It took some time getting started writing today. I nearly forgot everything I'd already written, so I needed to read through my previous entries. I think I know what needs to be said now. I need to tell you about her.

Her name was Elizabeth Catherine Moureen, or at least that was her name before she married me and adopted my last name. She was the love of my life from the moment I first laid eye on her. Of course, at that time, I was just a dumb eighteen-year-old kid without any real ambition. I was playing guitar in an uninspired rock-and-roll band, and Liz stood out at one of our debut performances. She bopped her head along to the music at the front of a less-than-impressive crowd. We shared a sort of magnetism. My eyes found hers without ever having to try, and they never really left.

I sought her out after the show. Her best friend (who later slurred her way through an overly enthusiastic toast at our wedding) showed greater interest in me and my band-mates, but I sought the admiration of the woman that caught my eye first.

Eventually, after wearing her down, she finally threw this old dog a bone. A week later, we went on our first date, although it was nothing worth writing home about. I took her to a drive-in movie and was rejected when I tried to make a move on her in the backseat of my uncle's station wagon.

She saw something in me. Where I saw awkward indecision, she beheld untapped potential. That's why she never gave up on me, even after what some might call a mediocre first date.

Even now, I can still picture her piercing blue eyes looking back at me, with tangles of ebony hair curled over the slender slope of her shoulders, and the sweet sound of the words "I love you" whispered in my ear. To me, she was the perfect vision of an angel personified.

That's all gone.

Now, when she comes in the dead of night, creeping and dragging her ruined body in her stead, that face stands as a fractured reminder of the act that silenced the beating of her heart. No words pass between us. Only a knowing gaze from a face left unseeing carries us through to sunrise, as a pinkish ooze issues forth from the cavity that once housed the beautyful features of her face. Her once luscious black hair has been singed back from a ruptured scalp, and the quilt-work of deep, irreparable scars stands as a constant reminder of her torment.

These nights are all we have left.

June 13th, 2017

The journal entry for the thirteenth of June was nearly illegible upon discovery, written in a scrawling hand that more closely resembled a child's scribbling than any form of rational communication. The contents of this entry spanned over a dozen pages, but despite our best efforts, only seven words stood out in a neater, more stylized hand amidst a sea of nonsense. Those seven words are as follows:

Her. Forgiveness. Seven. Remember. Eyes. Dying. Shadows.

June 17th, 2017

What does it mean to truly die?

I keep asking myself this, getting all wrapped up in one of life's greatest mysteries. I think I may have found the answer, but I'm not sure you're going to like it.

As children, we often ask our parents that age old question: "What happens to us when we die?" They usually di-verted our attention away from giving it any serious thought, telling us things like: "You're too young to worry about death" or "We'll talk about that when you're older." That's only because they didn't know themselves. No one really knows for sure.

At least, that's what I used to believe.

Liz has been coming to me with increasing frequency as of late. She's been keeping careful watch over me. I think she knows what I'm trying to do here, and I don't think she approves of it. These secrets were always meant to stay between us, but I still feel the need to justify my findings.

Last night, I woke to her standing at my bedside. She touched one swollen hand to my face, almost lovingly, and it chilled me to the bone. That short instance of contact drew a bridge between two planes of existence.

That feeling embodied death in its most primitive form. I felt it across every inch of my being. The grim spirit inhabiting her body filled mine with a dread like none other. For a moment, with her ceaseless gaze bearing down on me, I thought death would carry me off into our shared oblivion.

I feel so tired now. I think I'll go back to sleep. It feels good to get this all off my chest.

I'm so sorry, Liz.

June 18th, 2017

The doctor called today. He wanted to schedule an appointment to see how I've been doing. I told him it wasn't a good time. He didn't sound pleased.

I need to be careful now.

The phone started ringing again at 7 o'clock on the dot. It was an old friend of mine from work. He wanted to check up on me, asking if I felt up to catching up over a couple drinks. I didn't, but I thanked him for thinking of me.

There are some good people in the world. I'm not one of them.

Shortly after Liz died, I took a leave of absence from my job. I couldn't maintain composure long enough to complete even the most menial tasks. My mind constantly buzzed and rattled, and the world itself seemed to be coming unhinged.

I never went back to work. I don't think I ever will. That's all behind me now.

Now, I have something more important that needs my attention.

June 20th, 2017

The doctor called three times today. I let him go to voicemail each time. He threatened to take more drastic action if I didn't return his calls. He still wants to schedule an appointment.

I'm not worried. Liz will take care of anyone that comes to the house. She has my best interest at heart.

I think my memory has begun deteriorating further. I'm not sure.

Maybe I'll go for a walk around the neighborhood. The fresh air might do me some good.

Liz doesn't like it when I leave. It seems to make her nervous. Maybe she thinks I'm never going to come back. She should know I would never leave her. I need her just as much as she needs me.

Speaking of Liz, something started growing out of the hole where her face used to be. It's some sort of bulbous red growth. I'm not sure what I can do for her. It looks so painful, and yet she never seems bothered by it.

I simply cannot bear the thought of her being in any more pain. I'll have to think of something.

For now, maybe I really will go for that walk.

June 21st, 2017

I couldn't leave.
She wouldn't let me.
I have to stay here.
I'm no longer welcome out there.
I am a shadow.
I am her shadow.
I am unforgiven.
Please let me go.

June 23rd, 2017

I've started hearing her voice in my head.

Up until now, the version of Liz that returned from her accident never spoke to me directly. I didn't think her capable of speech anymore. Now, somehow, she's been projecting words into my mind.

It first happened when I tried leaving the house a couple days ago. Her voice exploded inside my head the moment my hand reached to open the front door. I nearly toppled under the weight of such untapped emotion.

"Don't you even think about it!" Those words rattled around inside of my skull. *"You wouldn't leave me, would you?"*

Of course, I wouldn't. I would never dream of leaving my Liz. I just thought the fresh air might do my mind some good.

But what do I know?

I'm just a fool who knows nothing of this world or the next.

I'd better stay here with her, at least until we've figured out what's going on with the growth that's sprouted from the dark hollow in her face. It's been growing more rapidly. It's about the size of a grapefruit now. Sometimes it even seems to pulsate and grow before my very eyes.

I can't leave her alone to suffer through this ordeal. She needs me looking out for her.

Don't worry, Liz. I promise I won't let you down ever again. I love you.

June 26th, 2017

Why can't I remember the color of her eyes? It always seemed so important before. Now I keep drawing a blank.

I think they were brown.

Yes, they were definitely brown.

My beautiful brown-eyed girl.

She would never forgive me if she knew I'd forgotten the color of her eyes.

She can never know.

June 27th, 2017

Why does it have to be me? Why do I have to tell it? It should be one of you.

I'm not ready. I'm not ready to remember everything that happened.

Maybe tomorrow.

Yes, I'll make my confession tomorrow.

I'll keep on sleeping in the shadows tonight. I need just one more night with her.

Please just give me that.

June 28th, 2017

She is Seven.

The Eyes are Seven.

The Truth is Seven.

Every story begins at Seven.

I'm not ready yet. Please stop asking me to go back.

I've pushed it all behind the shadows. That's where I live my life now.

I'll live with Liz by my side for as long as I can.

Please stop asking me to bring it all to an end.

I see the signs around me.

I see that number watching me.

The Answer is Seven.

My Life is Seven.

I will never tell. You can't make me. You can't make me go back to that day. It would break me. It would ruin everything I've built with her.

We need to forget.

June 29th, 2017

I've been doing a lot of thinking, and I know what I need to do.

Just not yet.

I'll tell you everything tomorrow. I just need one day to prepare.

June 30th, 2017

I started writing this several times over the last couple days, but I just couldn't seem to get my thoughts straight. I just hope I'm making the right choice.

The accident was something neither of us could have ever seen coming. It became something so profound and full of complexity that the landscape of our lives changed in ways I could never even begin to explain.

At first, I said I didn't want to talk about it, but I changed my mind. I think it needs to be said. I need to be honest with myself and with Liz.

The truth is

Wait, I can hear Liz calling me from the other room. I'll need to pick this up later. She still needs me.

June 2nd, 2017

Ever since I decided to be honest about everything, Liz has been angry with me. She says I can never tell anyone what happened on that day. If I tell anyone the truth, they won't let us be together.

I'm sorry. I need Liz in my life. I can't risk losing her again. She's all I have left.

The truth is something that will die with us. I won't betray her again, not after everything I've done.

This is the price of having her back in my life.

July 4th, 2017

Some of the neighbors are celebrating the holiday. They've been shooting off fireworks all night. I just wish they would keep it down.

I turned off all the lights in my house. I didn't want them to know I was home. I just want to be left alone.

But I can never be alone. Liz is always here with me. She's always watching me. She thought I was trying to escape the other day, so now she never lets me out of her sight.

I just want to be alone for a little while.

She's even looking over my shoulder as I'm writing this. She knows my every thought. Our pain is shared.

It needs to end soon. I'm not sure I can keep going like this.

The growth on her face is about the size of a watermelon now. It's started changing from a vibrant red to a sickly green color. I think it's going to pop soon. I just hope it doesn't hurt her.

I need to sleep. I just wish they would keep it down outside. It's been a long day.

July 5th, 2017

Liz has been growing more agitated with every passing day. I can't get her hate-filled voice out of my head.

She keeps talking about the accident, even though she won't let me talk about it. Her words have me reliving that day on repeat. I'm trapped in a never-ending loop, consumed by the pain of remembering every excruciating detail.

I think her voice has become warped.

I can't remember exactly how her voice originally sounded, but I know the voice I keep hearing in my head isn't the voice of my Liz. This voice belongs to the monstrous woman that haunts my every waking moment. She's the Liz I left broken, and I think she's still breaking even now.

Maybe it's the hideous tumor growing out of her face that's corrupted her, or maybe it's just a part of being dead. Who can say for sure? Maybe death changes you into a heartless embodiment of all the hatred you held for those that betrayed you in life.

In that case, I suppose it won't be long before she comes for me.

July 6th, 2017

The tumor didn't just pop. It exploded, sending a geyser of yellow pus raining down over the walls and ceiling of our bedroom. Every surface in the room was painted in the carnage that followed. Seeing it happen first hand took me back to that day. It was like watching it happen all over again.

I spent the rest of the day over the toilet, vomiting up what little solid food I'd managed to eat recently. I mostly just deposited mouthful after mouthful of stomach bile. It left a rancid taste in my mouth.

Only then did I start to realize how much I'd actually forgotten.

I can't remember my Liz's face anymore. The memories of our time together are twisted up into a nightmare. Now, every memory showcases a faceless wraith, with the bloody remnant of a pus-filled sack hanging from one festering eye socket.

The image of her like that is all I have left.

When I later returned to the bedroom, I found the house vacant once more.

Liz is gone for now. I don't know where she's gone or for how long. At least I'm alone. I think I need some time to think. Everything has gotten so out of hand.

I'd better go clean up the mess. There's no telling when she might come back. I don't want her to think I don't care about her.

July 7th, 2017

She's coming for me now.

I'm not crazy. I know I'm not crazy, but I am afraid. I'm afraid to be alone, and I'm afraid of living with the weight of my actions.

It's too late to turn back now. Liz is coming. I'm out of time. I'm prepared for the end. I'll embrace it now in these final moments of my life.

I can hear her coming. I can hear her voice in head. She's not happy. She remembers what I did to her, and I do too. That's the one thing I will never be able to forget.

It's my greatest sin.

She will knock seven times before entering. Seven is the mystic number. It's the cursed mark hanging over my shoulder and the noose I was always meant to hang upon.

That number will usher me into damnation.

Jamison John Hewitt was discovered dead in his home on July 7th, 2017, after a concerned neighbor reported what sounded like an argument taking place. That neighbor, who wished to remain anonymous, attests hearing two distinct voices coming from the Hewitt residence. The first voice belonged to the deceased, but the other had a gruff, inhuman nature (as the witness described it). The identity of this unknown individual has never been confirmed, although we suspect the voices were one and the same, with the second embodying a branch of Hewitt's madness.

Upon reporting, officers found Jamison John Hewitt dead on the scene. Hewitt had slit both wrists and was seated in a darkened corner of the home's master bedroom. A pair of razor blades were located beside each of Hewitt's outstretched hands. A handwritten journal was also recovered in close proximity to the body, soaked in the deceased's blood.

We have attempted to digitize the entries of this journal to the best of our ability, but some segments were lost or distorted. There are even indications that some pages were torn from the bindings of the notebook. None of these entries have ever been located in our search of the property.

Hewitt's suicide occurred exactly one year after his wife was pronounced dead. For more information on any connections between the two incidents, please refer to the case file on the disappearance of Elizabeth Catherine Hewitt. As of writing, no clear evidence has been found to connect Jamison with Elizabeth's disappearance, although some of the passages contained in his journal have resulted in a reexamination of our previous investigation.

Some believe those writings were the work of a man driven mad with grief, but in light of some recent happenings in Norris Township, I believe something more sinister is at work. A number of similar incidents have occurred over the last seven months.

One particularly eye-opening incident resulted from a series of tragedies surrounding the Ricker Family. Investigations are still on-going in this regard.

In conclusion, I'm deciding to reopen investigations into any strange happenings that may have influenced Jamison John Hewitt's mindset in the days leading up to his death, as well as renewed search efforts into the whereabouts of Elizabeth Catherine Hewitt.

In deepening our knowledge of these tragedies, I'm hoping to protect the public from further incident. Yet, I find myself afraid of what we may find.

-Norris Township Police Chief, Raymond Hampshire
February 7th, 2018

Foreshadowing

Garth Holmes slid the glass back and forth, from hand to hand, eyes growing distant. In reality, those eyes sought another world entirely.

As he sat, bathed in the artificial light of his laptop, the realms of his imagination rose to the surface. This was how he chose to unwind from the hardships of manual labor, in preparation for the slumber that seemed well-deserved in comparison.

The contents of the glass sloshed from side to side. This act resembled the steady wavering of a pendulum in ceaseless motion.

Lowering his eyes and relinquishing his hold on the glass, his hands moved forward to position themselves at accommodating points on the keyboard. The rhythmic tapping that followed served to slowly fill the white void with words flowing free of that other reality. Without stopping, new life took form within that digital space...

One of the woman's eyes hung from its socket, only still attached by a thread. She craned her head back in admiration of her assailant.

He wore and exuberant grin, splitting the corners of his mouth at a crooked angle. That look conveyed an underlying insanity.

Bearing an iron club in one hand, he barely allowed her the chance to recognize the source of her agony before bringing the blunt end down once more. He beat her bloody, until only an unrecognizeble mound of flesh remained of her once beautiful face. Blood and dislodged teeth scattered in every direction.

She fell at his feet, lifeless except for the occasional twitch.

Thin streamlets of sweat broke across his brow. Stepping back to savor the splendor of his work, he deemed the night a success.

Likewise, the man seated before his freshly inhabited word processer leaned back in his chair, looking over the spoils of his innermost venture. He seemed altogether unaffected by this grotesque conclusion, instead finding a sense of accomplishment in its completion.

Garth downed the last heated swig, draining his glass, before clamoring to his feet and departing for the comfort of his bed.

Dim light continued to fill the small makeshift office. The woman's miserable end stood in bold letters upon the screen. Its presence persisted into the small hours of morning, when the first blood-soaked spark of dawn intruded through the adjacent window.

Halfway through the next morning's first cup of coffee, Garth unfurled the daily newspaper, laying it flat across the kitchen table. The headline exclaimed a shocking realization: **"Killer on the Loose!"** At first, it seemed so in-your-face and exaggerated, that it almost sounded comical.

He delved into the contents of the accompanying article. It read as follows:

Late last night, the body of a yet unidentified woman was discovered behind the York Bottling Company's Distribution Center. The night watchman, Frederick Lemare, discovered the woman's remains when investigating the source of a commotion outside the Distribution Center's loading dock.

The commotion in question turned out to be nothing more than a territorial dispute on behalf of a group of stray felines, but in the process of chasing them off the property, Frederick made a more horrific discovery. The victim was beaten beyond recognition and concealed behind a dumpster at the back the building

Police have yet to reveal any potential leads into the identity of her attacker.

Many York residents fear a killer may be on the loose in their town. As this story continues to break, we advise residents to be wary of their surroundings in the nights to come. Police are urging citizens to report any strange sightings in the vicinity of Walter and Maribell Street between the hours of 12AM and 3AM last night.

Garth's brow furrowed. With arms crossed, he pondered this strange coincidence.

A killer on the loose in the peaceful town of York was entirely unprecedented. Even minor fender benders and domestic disputes were uncommon among the locals, and most were cleared up without the need for police intervention. In that way, the residents of York might even consider themselves placated in the calm of the mundane.

The York Bottling Company's Headquarters and Distribution Center were only a block from the automotive repair shop where Garth worked. He would actually pass the fenced in lot that housed the dumpster in question on his way to work.

Pondering the surreal qualities of this incident, his eyes drifted up to the digital readout on the microwave. He sat bolt upright, leaping onto his feet at once. At this rate, he would be late for work. He could offer no further consideration for matters that were outside his control.

Sprinting for the door, he departed for another day of his unnoteworthy life.

After returning home that evening, Garth prepared a dinner of frozen pizza.

The grisly murder of the woman now identified as Shirley Harper was the talk of the town. He could hardly get two words in either way, as every conversation veered off in the direction of conspiracy.

"Who do you think did it?" Albert Merle had asked him over lunch. Having not so much as the faintest idea of an answer to that question, Garth found himself growing agitated by the constant conversational shift in favor of this still unfolding mystery. "I know a guy whose wife goes to the same hairdresser as Shirley Harper," Albert went on without noticing Garth's annoyance. "He says she was always a nice gal. The quiet type that tended to keep to herself." Albert almost seemed to believe talking about it somehow made him a part of the story through association.

Everyone seemed determined to add their own personal flair to the known facts. Each retelling conveyed a sense of originality, even if no one really knew what to make of it.

Garth wanted no part in any of this speculation. He found it all so absurd that such a deep fascination could arise from a singular event that bore no relevance to any of their daily lives. In the process, he found himself drawing a divide between himself and the gawking masses.

After eating his meager meal, Garth retreated into his den of creativity. Seated before his laptop, his eyelids soon drooped to half-moons, barely perceiving the words ushered into existence through the pulse of his fingers.

These were stories he would never share with the world outside this room, but in the heat of the moment, they seemed to breath a life of their own. That night's tale built from the last, growing in stature, and becoming a legend in its own right…

Men clad in uniforms bore down on him, guns raised. A spotlight shone all around him, elongating his shadow against the brick structure at his back.

"Don't even think about moving," one of the uniformed men boomed in an electronically amplified voice from behind the line of first responders. This man conveyed a sense of superiority. "If you even twitch your finger, we'll open fire." That was a promise he hoped to keep.

The voiceless killer seemed unfazed by all this. He stood his ground even as police closed their circle around him. There were at least a dozen guns trained on him, and maybe even more from the looming structures that surrounded their gathering.

The suspect took one step forward.

"I repeat! Do not move or we will shoot!" The commanding officer's robotic voice bellowed into the night. A certain nervousness hid beneath its surface, resounding with only half-hearted conviction.

The killer's resolve was steadfast. He never so much as blinked an eye at their threats.

When their ensnared prey took another step forward, an initial warning shot cut loose. He seemed unfazed and not troubled enough to work himself up to anything above a brisk walk.

A rookie officer fired off the first shot actually meant to hit home. His body jerked clumsily as the killing tool in his hands sprung to life.

Others followed his example.

Bullets rained down over the young man. They appeared to hone in on their target without fail. The steady drumming built to-

ward the confrontation's penultimate climax.

No one present would ever forget the events that followed. One of the survivors would later describe the experience as "terrifying beyond belief."

The rattle of gunfire drew to a close as suddenly as it began. In the short silence that followed, they could hear crickets chirping from the high grass, while the young killer, who took an unsuspecting woman's life just one night before, stood surrounded by the littered remains of innumerable projectiles. Each bullet lay crumpled like wads of paper upon the pavement at his feet.

Their prey stood perfectly motionless. No bodily harm would come to him that night. Try as they might, the full force of the local police department proved powerless in putting him down. He was a monster of their own creation, after all. This man—if he ever was a man to begin with—represents their every mortal sin, with a few extra thrown in for good measure.

His body began to quake and tremble, as the town's keepers of the peace stood in disbelief at their inability. The body of the young man standing before them seemed to flicker out of existence momentarily. When he appeared once more, he no longer bore the unmarked skin of youth; instead, thick tufts of fur were beginning to sprout from every inch of his body. He lunged at their ranks before they could fully fathom the extent of his wolf-like transformation.

The commanding officer, safely poised behind a wall of bodies, watched with bleary eyes, as two of his men were torn clean in two. Their innards rained down around him, soaking the ground even before their bodies dropped.

Another seasoned veteran, toward the middle of the pack, raised his firearm in defense. Before he could pull the trigger, his arm was sheared off from the elbow down. His decapitated head would follow only a second later.

Five others died in an equally gruesome fashion.

The beast set his sights on the leader of their misguided troop.

This man promised swift action in the face of an unwillingness to surrender, but now he stood with his knees knocking together and a childlike terror contorting his features. This middle-aged man (far from a specimen of superior physique) had but a moment to peer up into the pitted eyes of the wolfman before having his still beating heart plucked from his chest. The wolf held it up for him to see.

His heart gave one final, pulsing throb, with thick claws digging deep rivets into its spongy surface. Realization filled the commander's eyes just before they glazed over. He dropped at the wolf's feet, becoming nothing more substantial than a sack of meat.

Fifteen local law enforcement officers responded to apprehend the suspected murderer. Less than half would live to tell the tale...

Garth was shocked to learn that three hours had passed in what felt like the blink of an eye. He hurried off to bed, counting the short five hours of sleep he would get before the labors of a new day would begin.

With thoughts of the wolf still playing out in his mind, Garth drifted off to sleep.

Garth would spend most of the following day walled in behind an insurmountable exhaustion. The day passed at a snail's pace, with him only providing the bare minimum toward the expected workload. The very act of breathing taxed him to his limits.

At lunch, his coworkers were once again overcome by a certain air of excitement.

Albert Merle turned to Garth with a wide grin. "Did

you hear something else happened out by the old sawmill?" he asked. "No one seems to know for sure, but they say the entire York County Police Department was seen heading out that way last night."

Only a sort of half recognition permeated Garth's sleep deprived brain.

"I bet it has something to do with whoever killed that girl," Albert went on, never seeming to notice his words were falling on uninterested ears. "To think, two nights of excitement in a row. It's unheard of."

Garth shied away from the town's insensitive way of thinking. In York, a woman's murder boiled down to a fair bit of excitement. The woman seemed all but forgotten in light of these new happenings. She went from being Shirley, the quiet girl that kept to herself, to becoming an overinflated avatar of their sick fascinations. Somewhere in translation, true matters of concern became muddled behind a wall of gawking on-lookers.

Garth wondered if maybe, deep down, they actually hoped more victims would appear before the plot's resolution; at least then they would have more talk about in the days to come. That thought made him hate the whole damn town and himself in the process.

He needed to end this. Later that night, he would lay it all to rest, putting this whole sordid mess behind them. Only then would he be able to go on with his life.

He would end it the only way he knew how.

They found the wolf face down in the gutter. A milky foam bubbled from between blackened lips. A large protrusion bulged and pressed against the inner lining of his throat, and upon further investigation, they would find a small bone lodged there. After the reign of terror that arose in the wake of his first appearance, the wolf died as a consequence of his own bottomless appetite.

Following the shootout that left the local police force in shambles, an epidemic of missing persons flooded the county.

Children became his new bread and butter. They vanished off playgrounds and while waiting for the school bus in the early hours of morning. Communal searches scoured the surrounding wooded areas, but not so much as a trace of the lost children were ever found.

Until now.

After local law enforcement failed to apprehend the criminal at large, a special investigative team took matters into their own hands, deeming the case extraordinary. No one could leave or enter town limits without a thorough check. The matter of the wolf became classified to the utmost importance. Should the townspeople learn the truth of the predator in their midst, mass hysteria would ensue.

In the autopsy that followed, the bone fragment lodged in the wolf's throat was removed and thoroughly analyzed. It originated from one of the wolf's latest victims. Thomas Harris, age 9, went missing two days prior to the discovery of his then deceased attacker. Through the loss of his life, Thomas at least ensured that he would be the last.

Some may call the beast's final moments anticlimactic. Though, in the grand scheme of things, it seemed somehow fitting for one such as he. To die alone, writhing and gasping, served a justice unlike anything those high-and-mighty gunslingers could dictate.

The remains of several of the other missing children were

found among the contents of the wolf's stomach, attributing every
recent disappearance to this creature's insatiable hunger.

At last, the case drew to a close.

The disappearances stopped altogether. Peace returned, even
as the town mourned the passing of those caught up in this bizarre
incident. Yet, in time, the memory of these happenings would fade,
and the town would fall silent once more.

Heaving a contented sigh, Garth felt relieved to know
that was the end of it.

The killer was dead. His remains were locked away in
some top-secret government facility. End of story.

Now he could rest. Tomorrow, he suspected life would
return to normal, never realizing the story had already grown
larger than he could ever imagine...

Closing his laptop, the room faded to black. The world
painted on his blank canvas flickered from existence, but continued to linger at the back of his mind.

A floorboard creaked in the still hours of night, drawing him back from the shallow depths of sleep. Garth sat bolt
upright. He felt someone's presence there. The thought made
his hair stand on end, and he imagined his ears even detected
the subtle whisper of their breath.

Out there, somewhere, the source of his misery
watched with eyes unafflicted by their sightless enclosure.
With breath growing short and labored, Garth spoke his
thoughts aloud: "You can't be here. I killed you. You had your

moment, but now you're dead."

The response that followed bore an unflinching edge. "No...You cannot kill what you do not understand." A young man stepped forth from the shadows. He was no wolf, but the wolf's presence lingered in his eyes.

Bedridden and afraid, Garth shrunk back from the sight of his own creation. The man seemed to change before his eyes. In one moment, he appeared as the young killer that took a club to a defenseless woman's face, next he morphed into a wolf-man hybrid, standing at least eight-feet tall, before flickering back into manhood. Garth's eyes struggled to pinpoint the monstrosity's true form, instead alternating between the maniac and the wolf contained within.

"You really thought you could kill me?" The wolf's words issued forth in a growl. "I've become more than just your puppet."

The idea of the wolf had grown beyond the comprehension of Garth's foolish imagination. He could no longer extinguish the words of fancy that flowed freely to the masses. Now, those ideas belonged to those who grasped their deeper meaning, giving them a life of their own.

He tried to kill the wolf, but the beast returned stronger than ever.

Raising one talon strewn paw, that momentarily seemed to linger somewhere between an animalistic killing tool and the blood-soaked hand of one who rejoices in the suffering of others, the wolf offered him one final quandary: "Do you know what happens now?"

"Yes," said the author. "Yes, I know what happens now."

The Down and Out

Martin stood with his back to her. His temper seemed to radiate through the room. She imagined she could almost see waves of heat billowing out around him.

He was in one of his moods again. It came as no surprise to her, not after years of marriage. More often than not, he returned home from work with a sour taste in his mouth. The troubles of his day quickly became her troubles, since his aggravation often lashed out without warning.

"I'm going out," he told her, trying to sound collected amidst the emotion lurking beneath the surface.

She knew she should just stay silent, already knowing the answer to the question that followed. "Going out where?" She sounded nonplused and on the verge of an outburst of her own.

"Just out," he responded curtly. "Don't you worry about it."

He was already opening the door. A cold winter wind cut through the home. Standing in the passage between the entry hall and the dining room, she wished that wind would carry her away, back to the fairy-tale ending she always envisioned.

He left without another word. She stood and watched him go, wordless and disbelieving how far they had fallen from the nights of romantic dinners and heated embraces between the sheets. Martin never so much as looked back before letting the door slam in his stead.

Standing there awhile longer, she thought of all the things she wanted to say to him. She lived in silent ignorance to the abuse of a loveless man.

Martin never hit her, not physically at least—even he would never sink that low. Instead, their marriage stood in barren terrain, where even the weedy underbrush withered and died. Her presence seemed burdensome to him, and he denied her even the time of day.

As she turned back to the dining room table, her eyes fell upon the untouched meal she prepared for him. It changed into something grotesque and hideous in acknowledgement of her own foolish intent. Maybe she would just never learn. She seemed fated to make the same mistake time and time again, or so she would tell herself night after night.

On shuffling feet, she moved to the side of the table. She bore the look of a woman caught in a trance. Reaching for a platter of fried chicken, she turned and flung it at the wall. The plate shattered and the meat tumbled to the floor, where it lay forgotten until common decency compelled her to clean the mess.

How much longer would she need to endure this psychological torture?

Later, as she knelt to clean up the shattered remains of the plate and the cooled lumps of meat, tears cascaded down her face. They burned there, and her heart ached for release.

After cleaning up, her mind switched into autopilot. She headed for bed, feeling like a wraith trapped in her own body. She vowed to bring an end to this nasty charade the very next day. Determined to unleash all those heinous thoughts filling her head, she rolled over and fell asleep, where her troubles followed into the fabric of her nightmares.

The next morning rolled around, and again the loop started back at the beginning.

What seemed so important the night before—the promise of escape—seemed somehow more distant. She decided to give him one more chance. Maybe this time he would change his ways.

He never changed.

Their lives continued in this fashion, until they were both too old to remember the good old days. Soon, years of potential led to a dead-end street with no way out.

The cycle carried her to death's door. The heaviness of regret hung overhead. She never experienced the fullness of life, as the trap closed around her. Eventually the questions would cease, acceptance would give birth to complacency, and a dry desert settled in where a bountiful garden once flourished beneath the glow of a summer sun.

Thus, the story ends in lonely desolation, like so many that came before.

Life in the Rearview

I

The hardest part of telling any story is knowing where to start.

Let me apologize in advance for my lack of organization. I will try to keep it to a minimum, but I write how I think, and my thoughts tend to move a million miles a minute. This story is important to me, though, so I need to get it just right.

My life was one born in shadow. I thrived off fantasies that always seemed just out of reach, unaware that it would end in the arms of the woman who made the struggle all worthwhile.

Beginnings are hard...I've always believed that, even as a child of simple understanding.

Singular events can turn the tides of one's life in a multitude of differing directions, with a new sense of purpose stemming out from that one moment in time. Every decision builds off the last, bridging the gap between a limitless expanse of possibility.

Endings, on the other hand, are easy. They're absolute. True endings are inarguable. Juggled atop the hands of time's eternal jester, the moment when the dizzying array of spheres fall into the void stands without objection. Everyone who ever told a story, even of something as simple as a mundane visit to the corner convenience store, sets out with a distinct purpose in mind. All storytellers wish to reach a finite point where all lines intersect.

For me, this was that moment...

My life ended at the mercy of a fire-spitting dragon of manmade design. It reeked of gunpowder, and the air felt heavy as the aerodynamic shell pierced my body. In all the forty-three-years of my life, I never considered that outcome; the underlying meaning only became apparent when the spark we all take for granted started to fade.

This story ends at the hands of a lonely man who has yet to find his purpose.

Now, let me tell you where it all began...

II

I first laid eyes on my wife-to-be as a sophomore of Freely High School in Upstate New York. She transferred in at sixteen, while I was only fifteen, and although I didn't know it at the time, my subconscious gleamed the importance of our meeting from first glance.

Her eyes, as they first acknowledged me, were a mystifying shade of autumn gold. The excess confidence embodied within every smile fascinated me, and her brown hair seemed to flow as it wavered against the arch of her back. I could relate nothing comparable to that instantaneous attraction; after all, nothing up to that point had ever gripped my heart so tightly.

Allison Kaye moved to Freely after the separation of her parents. She would live the remainder of her teenage years in the care of her mother. Originally, she grew up in Brooklyn, yet she lacked the accent that so commonly accompanied those inhabiting that particular corner of the state.

I first gathered the nerve to speak to Allison in our third period Algebra class. Indecision always got the better of me in the weeks leading up to that day, and I had yet to even introduce myself to her. It should come as no surprise that our earliest conversations were nothing worth mentioning, but I suspect her keen senses tipped her off to my admiration very early on.

We started dating a year later. I remember sharing a kiss in a darkened movie theater—a first for me, but not for her—and awakening to the existence of a love that exceeded my youth. In actuality, I fell in love with Allison before I even understood the root of that sentiment.

To fully understand that concept, I must first explain the hardships of my childhood. It plays an important part in my upbringing.

I can't quite bring myself to say my mother never loved me, but our relationship seemed different from others. I think she resented me in some ways, but deep down, I don't think she ever wanted children.

My father died shortly after my second birthday. He succumbed to the dark elixir that consumed his every waking moment. One night, already in a drunken stupor, he neglected looking both ways, allowing himself to step out into oncoming traffic.

After the accident, my mother lost a part of herself. Even after years of abuse, she remained affirmed to the belief that my father loved her, even if he never exhibited those emotions. She stopped looking at me after that, most likely due to my features resembling those of my father. The already scant well of maternal love dried to the bare minimum, and I went through the early years of my life believing myself somehow inferior.

Love never came easy for me…Actually, I'm not entirely sure that's the truest assessment of my innermost affliction. I think I lacked an understanding of what it meant to love, so when Allison opened my eyes to those feelings, I became ex-asperated to the point that it almost consumed me.

Our chance meeting marked a point of no return in my story. Everything grew from that prologue, and my individuality started taking shape.

III

She told me I was standing still, while her path moved ever onward. I needed to find my life's purpose before she could commit to anything, or so she told me before bringing my dream of a future to a crashing halt.

I left my hometown at eighteen, shortly after graduating and immediately after Allison delivered that unrestrained commentary on my lack of motivation. She headed off to college in pursuit of a law degree, while my future looked uncertain. We were two very different people when it came to planning for the road ahead, and as it turned out, her ambitions were stronger than mine.

Looking back now, I know she made the right choice.

The night after we parted ways, I packed a bag of only the essentials and spent what little money I had on a bus ticket out of Freely. The first leg of my journey carried me southward. In the community where I'd been raised, Florida held high regards as an almost holy place, where people go to bask in the light of purity. I left home with those ideals in mind, possibly even seeking a divine intervention of sorts.

Many of the places I visited served no real significance, but the experiences that followed my departure ultimately shaped my future. Putting the past behind me, I decided to follow Allison's advice and search out some greater purpose.

Numerous odd jobs provided a barely livable income. My choice to temporarily settle down at any one place depended entirely on my ability to find work. In the process, I developed an adversity to staying anywhere for too long. I feared growing complacent.

One night, while leaving my latest gig as part of an after-hours cleaning service for an office complex in a small Georgia town, I met a young, barely teenage girl crouched against the building's back exterior. Dressed in the tattered remains of what might have once passed for clothes, she acknowledged my presence with eyes more akin to that of a cornered animal.

The weight of that past week's pay felt heavy against the front pocket of my jeans. I laid my livelihood at her feet. She hastily leapt at it, almost expecting me to have a change of heart. She clutched the currency to her much-too-thin chest, and I could read the accusation in her eyes. I left her there, without ever looking back.

I gave a part of myself for the betterment of another that night. At eighteen-years-old, the darker half of the world became apparent to me, rearing its ugly face in the form of a scarred and hopeless child.

That sight never left me; it would haunt my dreams for years to come.

IV

Two years later, I found myself staying in a small shoreside town, as one of the largest storms in recent history turned the surrounding sea into the embodiment of wrath. On the eve of that great storm, while the locals headed for higher ground, my young and foolhardy confidence convinced me that no harm would come my way.

Before the night was through, I found myself treading in water up to my knees. One moderately powerful current could have easily swept me down into the depths.

The town itself seemed to vanish beneath this newly spreading branch of the Atlantic.

I did manage to reach safety before any serious harm befell me. My story would have had a very different outcome if not for the luck that saw me through that night.

In surviving this ordeal, my internal ideologies developed further, pushing me one step closer to something I'd been putting off for almost as long as I'd been adrift. I knew I could no longer cling to the idiotic beliefs of youth. I needed to rebuild many of the bridges I'd burned in setting my past aside.

For the first time in those two long years, I found the compass needle shifting my gaze back to where it all began.

V

I never did manage to mend the rift between me and my mother, yet when I returned for the first time in two years, the embrace we exchanged filled me with genuine warmth. It made me feel at home.

We spent the night recounting the events that followed my departure. Sitting there, I could feel the shadows of my past creeping up on me. I thought I could push it all away and start a new life, but the memories never stayed buried.

In searching for my purpose, I failed to realize I'd been looking in all the wrong places. It took a brush with death to make me see the truth.

I slept in my old bed that night. My dreams insistently brought me to the edge of an epiphany. I felt a strong desire to act upon this newfound motivation. The necessity to carve a new path eclipsed my past transgressions.

Allison's face, as I behold it on the day I first awakened to the potential for romance, continually rose to the surface. Some bridges were beyond repair, however. I cut off all ties with Allison after that fateful day. Any chance I might have had at rekindling the love we once shared died on the day I turned my back on her, and deep down, I knew I hadn't taken so much as a single step toward becoming a person worthy of her companionship.

As a laid there, looking out at the darkened shapes of a once familiar space, I recognized the vast distance between everything I'd once known. Fear brought me back, but my days on the road taught me nothing of the change I so desperately sought.

<u>VI</u>

I spent the next couple days under my mother's roof, but the longer I remained, the more I felt torn between two lives. Without even the slightest idea of where to go from there, I knew any thoughts of staying would prove counter-productive to my goals.

With renewed conviction, I decided to turn my attention elsewhere.

With Freely situated no more than forty-minutes outside the New York City limits, I decided to see what new opportunities might await in the big city. I'd been there once as a boy, but at that time, I found the constant hustle and bustle overwhelming. This time, I spent two days drinking in the sights of city life, with plans to set down roots for longer, maybe even seeking some new line of work.

The plan quickly changed, as a certain chance encounter caught me entirely off-guard.

I knew Allison had been attending school in the city, but I never expected to catch so much as a glimpse of her among the diverse social mayhem. Of course, I considered the possibility, but how could I rightfully believe I would even recognize her within the tightly packed throngs of people moving to-and-fro in their nonstop lives.

Some otherworldly act of irony had other plans for us, however.

On that day, walking a crowded New York City street, I became enthralled by the sight of a familiar Freely High School jacket draped over the frame of the woman I recognized from first glance. Allison walked with a hastened stride, clearly adapted to city life. Looking upon her now, the feelings I'd tried to drown in my absence stirred and radiated as strongly as ever.

Later that afternoon, I fled the city on a bus bound for the western horizon. Having found myself awash in wayward emotion, I made no attempt to convince myself of any great valor. Having seen Allison up close, I decided to never look back, with only my own stubborn pride to thank for this turn of events.

Everything I thought I learned in the face of pending doom fell on deaf ears, and I slipped back in with my vagrant ways.

VII

My father died in the grip of alcoholism, so up to that point, I never let so much as a drop touch my lips. My outlook on drinking never changed, but the bar scene brought an edge of exhilaration that made me feel more alive.

Over the next six years, I made the dark underbelly of the world my theater. In those lightless hours, I paid homage to the writhing sickness I first glimpsed in the starving face of a young girl in Georgia. At realizing the extent of the infection plaguing mankind, I found myself growing more cynical with every passing day.

Toward the end of my six-year stretch of isolation, a woman lost in the depths of inebriation dropped into the seat across the table from me. She wanted me to buy her a drink. I obliged, fearing for her safety in the hands of whomever she might ask next, and I ended up escorting her back to the motel

I'd established as a temporary home.

The hours that followed found our bodies bared and succumbing to our primal desires. Our lovemaking lacked passion. We simply gave ourselves over to our baser needs.

The next morning, I woke to find her dressed and sitting at the foot of my bed. As I sat up, she turned and offered a troubled gaze. "You're missing someone, aren't you?" she asked in a voice barely above a whisper. "I hardly know you…In fact, I don't even remember how I got here, but I can feel the pain that surrounds you." Her eyes turned away, refusing to look me full in the face. "My life is shit, but somehow, I know you've had it worse."

I didn't know how to respond.

Without another word, she gathered her things and departed for whatever troubled life awaited her. In her absence, I realized I never so much as asked her name.

VIII

It took word of my mother's passing to turn my listless sail homebound. Seven years had passed since we last spoke, and the guilt of that knowledge left a bad taste in my mouth. Unbeknownst at the time, those years of darkness, as a drifter lost in the wind, would draw to close upon returning to Freely.

From a careful distance, I watched them lower her into the ground.

There were several in attendance that day. I recognized some of their sorrowful faces, while others were unfamiliar to me. Standing in the shade of an ancient oak tree, I waited for the crowd to disperse before making my approach. The dirt had barely settled on her final resting place. I knelt over her and offered a word of thanks for all the hard days she endured in the face of adversity and grief.

I never truly understood my mother. She showed no outward affection, yet she always provided for me. Even when I returned, after severing all ties, she graciously accepted me back into her home. Thinking back now, I owed her an apology. My heart ached at knowing I'd stumbled on that knowledge too late.

My mother died alone, and I could do nothing to change that.

IX

I was always running away and never toward anything. It took the realization of my mother's abandonment to open my eyes to this inarguable truth. In my years adrift, I witnessed countless shadow-infested crevices, to which humanity more commonly turned a blind eye. The world proved darker than I would have ever imagined, and at some point, I think I lost myself there in those dark places.

I've come to regard the years since my first departure as an age of cowardice. I started running when I failed to recognize the potential Allison saw in me. At the time, I saw it only as a betrayal of the heart.

Trying to deepen my resolve in the wake of my mother's death, I visited the city once more. Last time, I felt the past encroaching on the false security I formed on my travels. Now, I needed to put myself to the test.

Going so far as to revisit the scene of my run-in with Allison, I sought some sign of my growth over the last seven years, taking an interest in whether that setting alone could cause a resurgence of the fear and uncertainty I felt on that day. The visit proved uneventful, but it got me considering my lack of understanding.

On some level, I think I'd been hoping to find her there once more.

I wandered the city for three days and three nights, never settling anywhere for long, but instead living as a piece of the backdrop. It gave me time to think.

Seven years earlier, some impulse drew me to the city. I turned my back on it then, but I've come to believe something more significant had plans for me there. As it happened, I just needed to embrace the ebb and flow of fate to draw me to my true calling.

Perhaps guided by the invisible fingers of the preordained, I found myself wandering into the lobby of an indistinct office building, seeking a reprieve from the sudden downpour outside. Seated away from the bustle of suit-clad businessmen coming and going at regular intervals, I planned to stay only long enough to see a break in the overcast sky.

That sanctuary proved more significant, however.

A secretary eyed me with uncertainty from behind a desk at the foot of a set of glass elevator doors. I saw her lift the phone from its cradle on her desk. She spoke with haste, eyes never moving from where I sat, and although I could hardly detect the hint of her words over the distance, I awaited the arrival of a security escort to remove me from the premise.

Several moments later, to my surprise, it was an older

man—passed the glory of youth, but not quite into his golden years—that appeared from the elevator at her back. He offered the secretary a brief greeting before meeting my gaze. Headed in my direction, he was dressed in a suit of charcoal gray, while holding a lightly swaying briefcase in one hand. He stopped in front of me, and I immediately recognized the presence of a distinct kindness amidst the tranquil blue of his eyes.

"Why the long face, my friend?" he asked, sounding genuinely interested. "The lines in your face tell me you have quite the catalogue of stories to tell."

"No stories here." My proclamation gave way to a short laugh.

"Now, now..." He grabbed a chair and situated himself at my side. "We all have a story or two to tell."

I thought long and hard on that sentiment, before finally deciding I had nothing to hide.

Seated beside the gray-haired stranger, I told him everything that conspired up to that point, starting with Allison and the foreseeable schism that drove us to opposite ends of the world. By the time I finished, I felt a sizable weight rising from the pit of off my chest. As the chain of events came unraveled, a deep sense of absolution took up residence in my heart.

As the words spun off my lips, time passed unnoticed. Now, the surrounding lobby stood vacant, and the streets beyond were aglow with the city's frivolous nightlife.

My new acquaintance sat in silence awhile longer, mulling over the finer details of my exposition. When he spoke for the first time since the start of my tale, his voice bore a melancholy edge. "You've experienced a great many things for one so young." He hesitated for a moment, seeming on the edge of some realization. "I, too, know of the darkness lingering behind the scenes of our society. I feel this introduction is now long overdue, but my name is Harley Janice." Harley extended his hand as a tangible exchange of our newly forged bond.

"You see, I'm an entrepreneur of sorts," he went on. "I built my business from the ground up, and I'm what you might call an interested party in bettering the present state of affairs. My experiences are fewer than yours, but I've always wanted to make a difference."

That caught me off-guard. I hadn't expected him to gleam any real significance in my story.

"If, possible, I'd like to hear more of your thoughts on how we can work at creating a better future." Harley placed heightened emphasis on the use of the word "we."

"What are you suggesting?" I asked, expecting the reveal of some ulterior motive.

"Maybe nothing," he answered plainly, without restraint, "or maybe a partnership of sorts." Harley considered his words more carefully now. "Most corporations seek to smother the secrets of the underworld and the suffering that exists beyond the gates of Capitalist America."

I waited. The pieces were beginning to snap into place.

"After hearing your story, I see a spark of potential in you. You've seen it for yourself. I need someone like that to keep me from losing my way." Harley Janice regarded me with a hardened gaze, in which I glimpsed a fire burning in the pit of his otherwise pure eyes.

"And what makes you think I'm that someone?" I never tried to hide my suspicions. "Maybe I'm just pulling your leg."

Harley shook his head and smiled. "No one pours their heart out the way you did only to turn back on their own ideals. You're exactly the sort of person I need as a second-incommand, and from what I gathered, you're looking to start over."

My head lowered. Even through my obvious uncertainty, this complete stranger chose to believe in something greater than either of us. I could feel him peeling back the layers of my past.

Finally, I raised my eyes to meet his. "I'd like to try..." A jolt of excitement accompanied my anticipation at what a partnership of this magnitude could mean. "But there's something I need to do first." I surprised myself with that, settling on a decision I'd been keeping by the wayside.

Harley nodded his head, as if already aware of the task at hand.

Before I could fully embrace this next stage in my life, I needed to close the book on my greatest failure.

X

I needed to make a call that was long overdue.

What savings still remained to my name were further hindered in the act of renting a hotel room that overlooked the stretch of concrete jungle where I last laid eyes on Allison. It needed to be there that I conquered my obsessive doubts.

Finding her last known phone number through the magic of the internet, I paced the length of the room in a desperate ploy to muster my courage. As the dial tone filled my ears, I nearly dropped the phone.

After what felt like an eternity, her voice chimed in from across an indeterminable distance. "Hello?" she spoke with calm clarity, oblivious to the waves of nostalgia coursing through me.

"H...Hey..." I could hardly form the words through a mouthful of sand. "Do you still remember me?"

At first, only silence punctuated my inquiry. I felt sure she had hung up, until her voice returned with the same unwavering composure. "Of course, I remember you, David. How could I ever forget?"

I had so much to tell her, so many confessions to make, and yet the words seemed lost behind a veil of indecision. I swallowed back those rising concerns and dove headlong into a shortened retelling of my story. Allison's reactions were hidden behind the mask of distance, and I could only hope she would at least hear me out to the end.

You might wonder what my intentions were, dredging up old feelings and forcing myself to face my mirrored regrets. I can hardly explain my train of thought, but at that time, I just wanted to prove my succession from foolhardy youth—without any inkling of the outside world—to someone on the pinnacle of breaking free. The confidence Harley imbued in me, accompanied by the promise of potential future prospects, pushed my determination into overdrive.

It was now or never. If I let myself slip back into the groove of inaction, I would never escape the repetition that followed.

Allison listened in silence, letting me tell my story. Once I arrived back at the present, stopping at the resolution of the unseen partnership with Harley, Allison spoke from the far side of the void. "Let's meet for coffee. I'll need to see your face to know if any of this is true."

I could feel my heart pounding in my chest. I'd planned to seal the affair and never look back, but Allison's words sent my mind reeling toward a new horizon.

"How does tomorrow at noon sound? I'm still living in the city," she continued, not giving me time to react.

"Noon works for me," I breathed those words in disbelief, securing a future I once thought lost.

<u>XI</u>

You already know how things end for Allison and me. I never sought to hide our eventual reunion, but believe it or not, I never intended this happy turnaround as the moral of the story.

Through and through, I set out seeking to illuminate my troubled soul and the transformation that conspired as the result of a series of events largely outside my control. I am human, as you will soon understand, and I have been flawed for as long as I've existed in this world, yet I followed a thin stream of light, piercing the darkest ravine of earthly decay, only to somehow wander back onto the path laid before me.

I have no intention of telling you all that conspired over coffee or the deeds of goodness that arose from working as a consultant to Harley Janice. You need only know the stepping stones along my path to redemption.

With that in mind, I think it's about time we get back to where this all began.

XII

Beginnings are easy, but that's all behind me now.

Everyone reaches a point in their life when they can no longer go back. I eventually found myself standing at a crossroads, with an insurmountable wall standing in my way.

I'm only now realizing that I never so much as told you my name—not directly at least. Thinking on it now, I'm not even sure it's really all that important. If you must know, most will remember me as David Hemming, while Allison and a few of our closest friends more fondly refer to me as "Davie." I find such matters trivial in light of what's to come, but the information felt necessary in completing the experience.

I've been putting this off for too long, dragging it out to prolong the inevitable. See me now, as I pay my final toll. At least, even in those final moments, I stood by my ideals and never wavered, even in the face of that dark tunnel.

We arrive now at these matters of discord and unraveling.

XIII

We were walking that same stretch of city street where I once caught sight of Allison in the years before I returned to my senses. Now we walked together, hand in hand, speaking on matters of importance in our lives.

Along the way, a man separated from the surrounding crowd. As he approached, I caught a glimpse of the blade concealed against the palm of his hand. It jutted outwards quickly, cleanly sawing through the leather strap of the handbag slung over Allison's shoulder. He snatched it up with grace and took off running.

Still as reckless as ever, I took off after him.

I distinctly remember the feel of my hand slipping free of Allison's insistent grip. She didn't want to let me go. Something felt out of place the instant I broke contact.

I bobbed and weaved through the crowd, trying to keep the man within my line of sight. He lunged off the sidewalk and into the street. I persisted in my approach, even as a car passed between us. As the intruding vehicle passed, fear stilled my pursuit upon recognizing the handgun that appeared from one of the oversized pockets in the man's jacket.

My mind raced at the sight of the muzzle trained in my direction. An earsplitting roar silenced those thoughts, followed by two additional thunderclaps.

A numbing coldness overwhelmed my other senses. My legs felt like rubber, and I toppled to the pavement below.

Even as I descended to my final resting place, I watched the young man—probably no older than when I'd left home for the first time—turning tail and running into the mouth of an alleyway on the opposite side of the street. I saw myself reflected in the frightened face of my killer. If not for Allison holding me to the mark, I may have even found myself walking a similar path.

There I lay, with the world seeming to blur in and out of focus around me. I became aware of a crowd forming in the distance, but somehow, I knew the emergency services would arrive too late to change the hand I'd been dealt.

Allison's screams, at witnessing my crumpled form, cut through the murmur of the crowd. She dropped by my side and enveloped me in her arms.

That's how I reached my moment of no return.

Before actually verbalizing the words taking shape in my mind, I practiced mouthing them in silence before speaking them aloud: "Never forget our story." I hoped she would catch them over the sounds of the city. I offered those final sentiments to the woman I learned to love in a time when love seemed improbable.

Like I said before, endings are easy. They come tightly packaged with a predetermined set of expectations.

As I drew my final breath, I considered the journey of my younger self. I found myself out there, amidst a storm of self-doubt and an inability to escape the fears of my past. Those experiences led me here.

I could not object to dying in her arms.

In the end, I found a life of love and happiness. I leave that for you to consider. Out of everything detailed here, I just want it to be known that I never gave up, and eventually, I found my way back home.

The Other Side

I could see the other hotel across the way from the window in my room. Three nearly vacant parking lots stand between us. On the outside, it appears all but identical to the hotel in which I'd been staying.

Each window in that adjacent building looms dark and lifeless, except for the one that lay directly parallel to my own.

The other me watches through that window. Even across the distance, I behold him with certainty, and I know he sees me through the same lens of clarity. He stands there, as naked as the day he was born.

He is me, just as I am him. This thought alone makes my head swim with an uncertain desire to retreat back into myself, all while wishing to scream into the face of the unknown, if only to hear the chorus echoing back across that unfathomable distance.

As I stand here, peering into the infinite, the void itself looks upon me with equal fascination.

Watching that other me, I catch a glimpse of the full picture. He's holding something at his side. I strain my eyes in trying to unravel the identity of that object. Then, his arm begins its sluggish ascent, almost in slow-motion. I caught the faintest glint off the object's metallic surface, as the light at his back lit upon it. He raises it higher still.

For me, recognition only strikes at the last possible moment.

The other me presses the muzzle of the gun to his head. Upon his face, I recognize the presence of an all-knowing grin.

He pulls the trigger.

A brittle click deafens me. It intrudes upon my every inner thought, causing me to flinch back from the window. I squeeze my eyes shut, and the sound erupts from somewhere inside my head.

When my eyes open once more, I find the world has

grown darker.

The other hotel continues to loom across the way, except now the windows are alight and painted by the hustle and bustle of the occupants within.

The light at my back flickers and threatens to leave me awash in darkness.

I look down, and to my surprise, the gun my doppelganger pressed to his skull hangs from fingers that now feel alien to me. The gun has an antique quality, like something out of an old Western. Its weight seems almost insurmountable.

Looking up once more, I see the other me in the window across the way. He seems somehow more real, and I find myself questioning my own identity.

The other me raises his hand and points in my direction. He wasn't pointing at me, but instead, his extended finger directs my attention to something looming at my back. That unseen force, hiding in my shadow, breathes a mote of frigid air that sends shivers racing up my spine.

I consider glancing back at this new tormentor, but I immediately change my mind. If I were to look, that would have been the end of it. The void lingers in my blind spot. If I am to behold its maddening gaze, my mind would come unspun at the seams, leaving nothing but a shell of a man.

I would not look. I would never move from this spot so long as that dark force lingers behind me.

The other me appears to be laughing, as if plucking each fearful realization from the surface of my mind.

Looking down, I realize the three lots that once stood between us were now gone. They were replaced by the absolute absence of light. Darkness reigns over this featureless terrain, spanning an eternity in every direction.

I have become that other me. The real me, poised naked

and triumphant, all the while laughing with glee, stands with light in full bloom at his back. He stands where I left off.

I find myself trapped on the other side of a mirror. The promise of truth only guarantees my unprecedented downfall. I have become a slave to my own temptations. Should I turn and look upon the world I now inhabit, I will find myself shattering across every facet of reality. I cannot bear witness to the world I now believe to be real, yet the desire to unveil the unknown burns at the back of my heart.

My dilemma bears an absolute burden, capable of breaking even the most resolute among us.

Looking down, I remember the gun. My grip tightens. Even knowing I should cast this instrument of destruction aside, I stand firm in my decision. I must escape this place by any means necessary.

Slowly, I raise the gun. Its weight seems tied to my desperation.

The other me finds this amusing. He knows what worked for him will not work for me in turn. I am real and he is not.

As I take aim, the expression on the face of the other me shifts toward something more akin to terror. He briefly waves his arms almost pleadingly, and his head jerks from side to side.

I pay his antics little mind.

Instead, I cock the gun and pull the trigger. It erupts with a fiery roar. An acrid burning aroma fills the air near my face.

The bullet hits its mark, sending ripples through the surface of the window. A webwork of cracks race out from the point of impact. The window hadn't broken entirely, but the bullet caused enough fragmentation to allow a warm summer breeze to escape the real world, bringing radiance to this cold, mirrored reality.

Something stirs at my back. My eyes grow wide as thin black tendrils pass on either side of me, seeking the fractured glass with a desperate yearning for freedom.

I look on as the other me presses his palms and then his face against the glass on his side of the balance. His eyes bulge from their sockets in watching the first stringy finger of darkness snaking its way through the hairline crack.

The lighted windows in the real hotel begin to first flicker and then darken one by one. An unsightly haze dulls my view, as more of the ink-stained mass forces itself into a world outlined in light. They're feeding upon that light, drawing it into themselves, until nothing remains of its luminescence.

A sense of calm washes over me. The last of the void passes through the cracks in the fabric of this reality.

With the abyss no longer standing at my back, I depart those vacant halls in search of a cure for this madness. I find only an inescapable labyrinth. I learned the hard truth of the universe.

Once touched by the abyss, you can never go back.

Merlin and the Brothers Three

Once upon a time, a wizard of great renown lived in a world not far separated from our own. That man would eventually become known as Merlin the Wise to some, Merlin the Wizard to others, while he knew himself only as a humble hermit, seeking to unravel the mysteries of the universe one thread at a time.

Merlin lived alone on the outskirts of a dark forest. Content at keeping to himself, away from the workings of man, his attention remained focused on the natural balance. He knew little of the advancements of the world outside his selective bubble.

Standing beside the makeshift hut he called home, the forest breathed a life of its own. A darkly unpleasant miasma rose into the atmosphere, collecting as brooding clouds of unnatural smog. The noxious air seemed to pour from every miniscule crack in the fragmented trees, rising toward the ever-darkening sky. The forest bore an oppressive aura. In all the time Merlin took up residence at the forest's outer limits, there were none brave enough to venture beyond the natural boundary.

Even he, as great as the stories would proclaim, feared the woods outside his doorstep. They stood in opposition to every law he knew as a quantifiable truth.

On some days, upon peering through the warped silhouettes of those skeletal branches, he imagined he perceived strange and huddled forms creeping through the darkness. They were the forest dwellers, as he came to know them, and their continued existence within the confines of that dark place perplexed him greatly.

Occasionally, Merlin would creep to the edge of the woods. Standing close enough to almost grasp one of those leafless branches, he squints his eyes against the absence of light. He hoped to glimpse one of those forest dwellers. When no movement catches his attention, however, he eventually returns to his humble abode.

Even so, he could not shake the uneasy feeling that rose in the pit of his stomach. For just a split second, he felt another presence watching him.

The scope of his earlier works may shine a light of comprehension on the fear Merlin felt at the prospect of this lightless terrain. This man once ventured beyond the walls of reality, into a world outside his own, to discover the source of all life energy, ultimately granting himself an overabundance of its bounty.

Merlin uncovered the secret of immortality at a cost. That cost had yet to reveal itself, but he could feel its eventual consequences lurking in the back of his mind.

In the end, Merlin would live to the ripe age of 7047. He would die in battle alongside a great many brave warriors, but that remained a part of an unseen future. While living on the edge of that dark forest, Merlin was but 347, making this only an offshoot of childhood in comparison to his heightened lifespan. He knew little of the universe then, but he would unveil many of its secrets in the years to come.

In his 347th year, Merlin discovered the secrets of friendship and heroism thanks to the efforts of three brave souls. They would change the course of his life forever.

At the crack of dawn one morning, Merlin awoke to the sound of voices outside his hut. He sat upright, listening and trying to catch a hint of their intent. He detected the intonation of three separate voices. They spoke with great fervor and a lightness of heart that only accompanies youth.

Merlin dressed himself in simple robes and emerged to see who dared trespass so close to the dreaded woods.

There they stood, the three of them all in brightly colored armor that seemed almost in jest. They were even younger than he expected. The youngest of their ranks appeared no more than a day over eighteen.

"Why have you come here?" Merlin asked, already prepared to turn them away from this dark place—for their sake and for his.

The eldest of the trio stepped forward. He appeared no more than twenty, with fair, autumn gold hair that billowed with the passage of a calm breeze. He wore a set of armor that glowed in the still morning sun, casting motes of turquoise blue in all directions. A matching helm bobbed in a strap against his hip. "We are but three brothers," the eldest spoke for their company. His voice embodied a confidence that surpassed his years.

"That tells me nothing of why you've come here." Merlin tried to keep his tone even. Years of isolation taught him nothing of social etiquette.

"We have come seeking your assistance," the eldest knight implored. "We have heard much of your deeds."

"Deeds?" Merlin almost scoffed at this. "I have done nothing worthy of such praise. I am but a very old man, who has done little to help others."

The youngest of the group broke formation. His armor radiated with a warm scarlet hue, while an underlying nervousness appeared in his features. "We would not ask much of you. Please hear our request."

The eldest brother fixed the youngest with a stern look, silencing him.

"No," Merlin spoke with an unwavering persistence. "I would hear what this young man has to say. I see truth in his face."

The youngest among them stood taller than his elder brothers. With long, brown hair tied back to keep it from falling into his eyes, he looked between the faces of his two companions. In those eyes, Merlin recognized a distinct quality, marking that youth as a person of particular interest.

The elder brother shied away from Merlin's disdain, as if somehow injured at the thought of being passed over for one of his siblings.

"Tell me your name," Merlin spoke directly to the boy, forcing him to maintain continuous eye contact.

The young man lowered his head and spoke in a hushed tone. "My name is Arthur, Sire. I herald from the wooded realm, out beyond the rocks to the south, along the curve of the cursed forest."

Merlin raised a pair of bushy eyebrows. "Arthur you say?"

"Aye, Sire." The young Arthur seemed taken aback at hearing his name reverberated back off the lips of the wise one.

"I have met others who bear that same name, and they've all proven themselves resourceful beyond their years. Shall I expect the same of you?" Merlin's interests seemed tipped in favor of this turn of events.

"Oh no, Sire!" This Arthur flushed a shade of red that matched the radiance in his armor. "I am but an apprentice knight, nothing less and nothing more."

Merlin shook his head, refusing to accept such an answer. "I find that very hard to believe."

The eldest brother chose this moment to interject once more: "Please hear us out! We have a request of dire importance to our people."

Merlin raised a hand to still his qualm. "Whether I take an interest in your plea will depend solely on how I judge your character. Thus far, I find you rather impulsive and thoughtless. Very unbecoming of a knight. You must remain calm and collected in the face of all danger. Only death awaits those who act before they think."

This stilled the elder brother's flagrant tongue at once. He appeared unaccustomed to such scornful words. Bearing the pride of natural talent, he expected the utmost respect.

"Tell me your name," Merlin asked the eldest brother.

"Me? I am Reynold," he replied, clearly surprised that word of his deeds had yet to reach the ears of this lonely hermit.

"And I suspect you consider yourself the captain of this merry band?" Merlin remained unconcerned by the increasing discomfort shone on the young man's face.

"Why, yes, I suppose you could say that." Reynold looked ashamed to admit as much.

"That is most unfortunate." Merlin sounded genuinely disappointed.

Reynold opened his mouth to speak, perhaps planning some retort in his defense, but Merlin raised his hand once more.

"And what of you?" Merlin looked to their silent, middle brother.

The soft-spoken knight stood with shoulders hunched. He was dressed all in brightly luminescent emerald, while brandishing a sword almost as tall as himself in an ornately decorated sheath, strewn across his broad back. His wild brown hair stood up in tufts atop a bulbous head. He shuffled forward and opened his mouth, considering his words carefully. "They call me Hayden."

Merlin imagined the size of his weapon might prove troublesome in actual combat, but it gave the squat and brutish knight the look of a fearsome barbarian in the making. He knew better than to underestimate the carefully calculated demeanor with which Hayden spoke. Merlin went so far as to suspect the intellect of their silent tail far exceeded that of the two more ambitious brothers.

"Tell me why I should consider your request, Hayden of the green lands beyond the rocky flat. I would hear your words, and perhaps then I will consider your request." Merlin sought to deepen his understanding of the bonds that held these three together.

"Our people are being attacked." Hayden got right to the point, not bothering to mince his words; Merlin liked that about him. "By night, a foul creature sneaks forth from beyond the shroud of the cursed woods, devouring unsuspecting villagers whole, while our every defense has proven powerless."

Merlin rubbed his palms together, slipping into the fold of thoughtful consideration. "A creature?" Mention of a creature lurking in the dark forest caught his attention. "What sort of creature?"

"By gods, it's a snake as large as a house," Reynold leapt at the chance to speak. "I even saw it with my own two eyes. It stands nearly ten feet tall, with fangs capable of piercing even the most well-crafted armor, and scales strong enough to shatter steel. How can we possibly hope to stand in opposition to such an abomination?"

"How indeed..." Merlin thought it through, recalling the hunchbacked shapes he saw moving through the shaded underbrush.

"Our village elder spoke of your incredible feats. He believed you might have something that could help us." Arthur's words became a desperate plea.

"Perhaps," Merlin answered at once, "but I make no promises until I've heard more of what you know of this creature."

They moved their palaver to the cramped interior of Merlin's secluded home. The three brothers found themselves seated around the hearth. The air felt heavy with the potential of their union.

Reynold, Arthur, and Hayden each took turns telling their third of the account of the night three days prior, when they attempted to defend the village against the serpentine threat. They failed utterly, and three more victims were claimed before the creature ceased its rampage. Their weapons proved ineffective at dealing even a scratch to the beast's steely hide.

"I don't know what else there is we could have done. We tried everything in our arsenal. Our people are going to suffer, and we're powerless to stop it." As he confided this, Reynold shed his former arrogance.

Merlin could not help but sympathize with their ongoing plight, knowing the importance of kinship from past experience. He ran his fingers through the thick black beard sprouting from the curve of his chin. "I see...This is most troubling."

"I tried fighting it off, but I barely escaped unscathed. It's something beyond all comprehension." Out of the three, only Reynold witnessed the creature first-hand. He tried to slay it, but his blade only shattered upon making contact.

"Then it's a very good thing you managed to escape. Your recollection is of the utmost importance. Tell me everything you remember of the creature." Merlin prepared to form a mental reconfiguration of every detail Reynold could recall from his encounter; that information would prove vital in preparing a course of action moving forward.

Reynold told him everything—every gory detail. Through this shared knowledge, a bond formed between Merlin and the three brothers.

"There's only one thing left to do," Merlin declared with certainty.

"There is?" Hayden, who rarely spoke, added his surprised input.

"Yes." Merlin nodded, and a smile actually touched his lips. "But first, we must make preparations."

"Preparations for what?" Reynold sounded equally dumbstruck.

"Preparations for our hunt. We'll need to track the creature's trail through the woods. It'll surely lead us to its nest, and the only hope we have of slaying the maneater is to catch if off-guard."

Arthur's eyes grew wider. "You can't possibly mean to venture into the woods; to do so is akin to suicide!"

"You are not wrong." Merlin turned his attention to an old chest inscribed with strange runes that seemed to glow in the light of the fire. "Would you rather sit back and await another attack? That seems foolish if you ask me. If we have the element of surprise at our disposal, we may well gain the upper hand."

The three brothers sat in stunned silence. They saw no fault in Merlin's logic, yet thoughts of venturing into the forest frightened them even more than the creature itself.

Merlin produced the first artifact from inside the chest. He held it up for them to see.

A small glass vial laid in the palm of his hand. Its contents shone with a golden glow that instantly illuminated every dark crevice in Merlin's hut. "Do you know what this is?" he asked the three of them, not expecting an honest answer. "It's pure starlight, snatched from the night's sky and encapsulated here for our viewing pleasure."

"What does it do for us?" Reynold asked, looking entranced by the brilliant light.

"Starlight cuts through even the thickest darkness. It will protect you from the poisonous air of the forest. Without it, you wouldn't last even an hour." He let the vial slip into the crease of his robe, where it would remain concealed until they had need of its protection.

Merlin hunkered down over the chest situated against the far wall. Its depths seemed limitless. "Arthur, come here for a moment. I have something for you," he called to the youngest of their party without looking up.

Arthur glanced to his brothers for some sign of reassure-ance before heeding the timeless wizard's call. Upon glancing over Merlin's shoulder, the treasure trove at their disposal appeared entirely empty. A second later, a bundle wrapped in blue velvet appeared out of thin air, as Merlin's hands emerged from inside the chest. He held it out to the young knight.

"Take it. You'll be needing it," Merlin told him, urging Arthur to push through his disbelief.

Arthur accepted the offering. The clothbound bundle proved heavier than he expected. "What is it, Sire?"

"It's a weapon of grave importance. I'm trusting you with it, but I expect you to return it once we've seen this through. Do you understand?" Merlin's nature turned suddenly serious.

Arthur nodded his head at once, although only half registering Merlin's words. A power pulsed through the cloth, coursing through his bare palms.

"Go ahead and remove the covering, but prepare yourself. It will feel like nothing you've experienced." Merlin maintained a grim façade. He wondered if he made a mistake entrusting this prized possession to the Arthur of this world.

Arthur seemed oblivious to Merlin's inclinations. He found himself mesmerized by the power placed at his disposal.

"What are you waiting for?" Reynold asked, snapping

Arthur back to reality.

Arthur stood up straighter and looked around, as if having just awoken from a dream.

"Take a look," Merlin repeated. Growing uncertainty showed in the lines of his face. He hoped this Arthur would not find himself consumed by that power.

Arthur scrutinized the bundle once more. He pulled the cloth covering free with one hand, being careful to balance the weight of the object atop the other. The protective material fell to the floor, where it lay forgotten, and the youth's eyes basked in the brilliance of the dazzling sword beneath. It appeared to be sculpted from some type of crystal. As the light of the fire hit the blade's opaque surface, it sent light refracting in every direction. Arthur fell in love with its beauty at once, and its hold over him grew stronger.

"That is a priceless artifact of the likes this world has never seen," Merlin informed the group, equally enthralled by the sword's beauty. "Its original owner slayed a mighty beast called a dragon in another place and time. He was also named Arthur, but that valiant king fell in battle long ago. I mourn his loss every day, and I see a little of him in you." He inclined his head to the still living Arthur. "I will lend you his weapon." Merlin's voice softened as he spoke of the Arthur he knew from days passed.

"What happened to that other Arthur?" asked the Arthur of this where and when. His eyes never ceased admiring the sword.

Merlin shook his head dismissively. "That is a tale for another day, and a long one at that. If we should survive, I would be happy to tell you of the man who overthrew the Lizard King with that mystical blade."

Arthur seemed interested in the story, but he understood the need for urgency.

Merlin shifted his gaze from Arthur to the lumbering Emerald Knight still seated by the fire. "Can you actually wield the blade you wear upon your back? It appears quite formidable." Merlin needed to know all the strengths at their disposal.

Hayden looked puzzled but nodded his head in acknowledgement all the same.

"Good, but I suspect it's not nearly as deadly as one might gleam from first glance." Merlin still seemed unconvinced.

"What makes you so sure of that?" Reynold spoke for his brother, clearly trying to press the bluff.

"Quality steel is a rare commodity in these parts," Merlin remarked knowingly. "What are the chances your small village chanced upon enough to forge a weapon of that magnitude?"

Reynold fell silent, suggesting a truth to Merlin's suspicions.

"I make do with what I have. You can count on that," Hayden spoke for himself, not wanting Reynold to stand in his defense. When push came to shove, Hayden's beliefs and loyalty for his family were unshakable. In time, Merlin would grow to regard him as a powerful leader in the making.

Merlin offered Hayden a smile. "Fear not. I never doubted your abilities for a moment. It's only the quality of your weapon I call into question." From within a pocket of his robe, Merlin produced what appeared to be nothing more than an ordinary stone, small enough to fit inside his balled fist. "Take this and hone your blade on its edge. You will find it works wonders on steel." He handed the stone over to Hayden and shooed him out into the yard, where he was instructed to sharpen his blade in preparation for the coming battle.

"Now, that leaves but one." Merlin stood tall, eyeing

Reynold with growing interest.

"What of me?" Reynold remained skeptical of Merlin's prowess, even as his brothers developed an underlying respect for their new mentor.

"You remain a puzzle to me," Merlin commented, stroking his beard quizzically.

"I see through your tricks," Reynold refused to hide his innermost doubts. "We don't have time for this. We need to help our people."

Merlin's eyes narrowed. He scrutinized Reynold's every feature, sizing him up in search of his most prominent trait. This proved difficult, as Reynold fought to keep himself closed off, but Merlin saw this as a challenge to overcome.

Finally, something snapped into place, and Merlin's eyes lit with dawning inspiration. "Ah-ha!" the wizard exclaimed, lifting his hand skyward. The billowing sleeve of his robe dropped away, revealing a surprisingly toned arm be-neath. He lowered his now clenched fist, turned it over, and spread his fingers. As if drawn from the air itself, a small fruit sat upon his palm.

By no means appetizing in appearance, the fruit looked rotten to its core, with deep crevices of infestation skewered throughout. The smell hit Reynold's nostrils at once, and he flinched back from the decaying matter without a moment's hesitation.

"What in the world is that?" Reynold held his nose, trying not to breathe in any of the noxious fumes.

"This?" Merlin moved the fruit closer to Reynold's face; the gesture made the eldest brother recoil in disgust.

"Get that away from me! Have you lost all sense?" A hint of green touched the pallor of Reynold's face.

"If you should partake in its succulence, your senses will be born anew." Merlin meant this as fact, giving no hint at any form of trickery.

"Partake? You can't possibly mean for me to eat that! It is surely poisonous."

"No poison here, my young friend. I only deal in the arcane arts of the white. I steer clear of the darker rites that poison the body and soul alike. I would never lead you or your brothers astray. I respect your virtues and seek to open a new way forward for you. Now take this, and then we will get on with matters."

Reynold looked Merlin in the face, searching for even the slightest trace of a lie.

Reaching out tentatively, Reynold took the rotten fruit in his hand. He held it there, feeling the damp and spongey exterior. With eyes squeezed shut, he raised the fruit to his lips. The stench filled his nose and made him gag uncontrollably. "Do I really have to?"

"If you wish to avenge your fallen brethren, then yes. If you wish to meet the same fate, then you're free to cast your lot without my assistance." Merlin's voice turned stern and unmoving.

"So be it..." Reynold took a deep breath. He bit into the rancid flesh of the fruit. It made his eyes water, and a deep heaving in his stomach attempted to reject the seemingly inedible.

"Swallow," Merlin instructed, allowing no time for questions.

It took Reynold three attempts to get the lump down his throat. The first two times, he nearly upended the contents of his stomach on the floor of Merlin's hut. On the third attempt, he barely got it down, retching loudly, as he clasped one trembling palm to his mouth.

"Good. Now open your eyes," Merlin continued to encourage his cooperation.

As Reynold's eyes opened, an unbelievable sight filled them with unmatched wonder.

"What do you see?" Merlin asked, already knowing the answer. He partook in that very same fruit more than a hundred years before.

"I see everything..." Reynold could hardly believe it.

"Do you see the color in everything?"

"Yes! Gods, yes! There's so much. It's so vibrant." Intermingling lines of color swam through everything. They appeared infinitely mystifying.

"This is the source of my trade," Merlin confirmed. "You're seeing magic in its purest form for the first time."

Reynold glanced down at where he held the rotten fruit. Now, a luscious apple of solid gold, with but a single bite removed, sat in its place. It almost seemed too perfect to be real. Driven by some undying impulse, he drew the apple to his lips to take another bite, but Merlin's hand lashed out with lightning quickness to pluck the radiant fruit from the young man's eager hand.

"That's enough," Merlin told him. "More than a single bite would drive you mad with a lust for power. I've seen it happen to great men before, and it never ends well."

Watching as Merlin flipped the apple into the oversized sleeve of his robe, Reynold nodded his head in unwilling acceptance. He felt robbed of greater potential, but understood the root of Merlin's concern.

"What did you do to my brother?" Up until now, Arthur watched this strange exchange with bated breath.

"I opened his mind to forces beyond his understanding. Perhaps one day you'll wish for the same." Merlin looked to Arthur with sorrowful eyes. "The fruit of the Tree of Adam inspires greatness in men, granting magic where none lived before. Young Reynold will need to hone this art, but in time, he may become a wizard in his own right." This exchange stirred the warm memories of Merlin's own introduction to the magical arts.

"But what can I do with it?" Reynold asked, glancing around at his newly invigorated surroundings.

"That I cannot say for sure." Something seemed to stir beneath the surface, and Merlin's eyes turned downcast. "Magic plays a different role for everyone. I hope you'll lead a life of unending heroism, but I've seen too many of my kin stumble from the path. They find the allure of the dark too overwhelming and throw themselves wholeheartedly into its embrace. This ends in death for most, but sometimes it proves worse still. I shan't speak of those unmentionable sins, not so close to our nearing battle, but those lost to the dark still exist in places far from here. Just remember, whatever you choose to do with the power I've granted you, it will leave its mark on the world."

A contemplative silence settled over them.

Arthur broke that silence, looking from his brother to the wizard who chose to rally at their side. "So, what do we do now?" He sounded small and distant.

They each considered the weight of the journey ahead.

"Now, we go to battle," Merlin spoke without looking at them.

How long had it been since last those words touched his lips? So many battles waged under his watchful gaze. In his time walking the many worlds of existence, great wars burned to extinction, men of much renown died to the sword, and others turned a blind eye to evil's lingering presence.

This Arthur reminded him of that other Arthur. King Arthur of Britannia died as his foe lay bleeding. His victory came at the cost of Merlin's most commendable ally. He would never forget that Arthur, but now he saw a fragment of his old friend in the burning desires of these three brothers.

"Into the cursed woods?" Arthur asked, sounding frightened despite Merlin's support.

"Into the cursed woods," Merlin agreed. "It is the only way, unless you wish to turn from your intended course."

"No! We shall not!" Reynold's voice rose in calamitous opposition.

Just then, Hayden appeared at the door behind them. He watched them solemnly, resolute in his silent demeanor.

"Then we should move while the sun still hangs in our favor," Merlin instructed, prepared to stand with these three unlikely heroes.

They all looked surprised and taken aback at his words.

"You plan to accompany us?" Reynold asked, not even trying to hide his disbelief.

"Aye. I would never think to send you off to battle alone." Merlin stepped forward. "I fight neither with sword nor shield, but this old man may yet prove useful to your cause."

Reynold bent his head in acknowledgement of the wizard. "We thank you for all you've done, but we do not ask you to put your life on the line for the sake of our livelihood." Since receiving his gift, Reynold's attitude changed wholeheartedly.

"Silence your foolish tongue," Merlin retorted at once. "I will hear none of your complaints. I have long planned to embark into yonder woods, and so you three will accompany me to the source of all this mischief."

The three brothers argued no more. They fell in line, and Merlin led their arrangement back out into the yard.

"How did thee fare?" he asked Hayden, shifting his gaze to the sword upon his back.

"It's hard to say, but the blade seems sharper than ever." Hayden followed at the back of their arrangement.

"Good. I fear you will have need for it soon enough."

Merlin led them to the edge of the forest. An untamed cropping of thorny bushes outlined the perimeter of the woods. Their pinprick tips leered imposingly before them. Should they venture through this deadly screen on foot, they would surely find themselves skinned alive.

"What should we do?" Arthur asked, inching an exposed fingertip toward one of the thorns.

Merlin snatched his hand back with haste. "Be not a fool, unless you wish to infect yourself with the poison of this place."

Arthur looked away abashedly.

"Fear not. I shall open a way through." Merlin held his hands out before him, palms outturned.

Reynold watched in amazement, as a dazzling array of color pooled outward from Merlin's hands, permeating the frightful thicket. The others only saw the thorn patch beginning to separate at its center, forming a path for them to travel into the darkness beyond.

"Now, as long as you're prepared in body and mind, we shall go." Merlin stepped forward, entering the woods without bothering to wait and see if they would follow. Each stepped in behind him, forming a single-file line.

Traveling deeper into the tangled maw of the forest, they struggled to see even a couple feet in front of them. In response, Merlin reached his hands toward the canopy of trees overhead. He spoke words they could not understand, and a small globe of light descended in front of them. It bobbed along the path, seeming to harbor some knowledge of their intended destination.

Even Merlin heeded the navigational awareness of his creation. He followed, eyes always vigilant and scanning the forest for even the slightest sign of movement.

An hour into their trek, a bout of sickness befell Hayden. He dropped to his knees, and his body spasmed violently. His eyes moved in frantic circles, trying to perceive the entirety of their surroundings all at once. "What are they?" he muttered in a vacant voice. "They're everywhere!"

"Who's everywhere?" Reynold bent and grasped his younger brother's broad shoulders. He gave Hayden a through shaking in an attempt to snap him out of whatever spell held sway over him. A dark aura surrounded Hayden, cloaking his form behind a haze of dense shadow. Reynold recognized the similarities between the magic swirling around his brother and that which emanated from Merlin's every miraculous act, except this magic originated from the darker half of the spectrum.

Arthur glanced around, hoping to catch sight of whatever troubled Hayden, but as far as he could tell, nothing of note peered back at them.

"Step aside." Merlin bent to examine Hayden's face. "The time has come." The golden vial of starlight appeared in his hand. Upon removing the stopper, he poured the richly glistening liquid over Hayden's brow. The stream sizzled and thin tufts of smoke rose upon making contact with Hayden's skin.

Slowly, the terror faded from Hayden's face, and he returned to his senses. "What happened?" He looked to them with unknowing puzzlement.

"The forest had a hold on you, but you should be safe now. The effects of the starlight won't last forever, but it should hold until our job is done. We should all bask in its glow now. We must stand ready to face the dangers still ahead." Merlin passed the vial to each brother in turn, having them christened in the light of a celestial body plucked from the night's sky.

With the rite of protection complete, Merlin returned the vial to the inner folds of his robe. They may find use for the remainder of its magic.

"What about you?" Reynold asked. "Won't you be needing any of its light?"

Merlin failed to anoint himself, only bearing it for the sake of the three brothers. "That will not be necessary," he confided. "I've bathed in the light of the stars many times before. It's in my bones now. I no longer need its protection to turn aside evil's influence. I need only rely on my own senses to keep me sane."

Just then, a branch snapped in the distance, drawing their attention. They turned and peered off into the darkness. Another crackle of dry earth signaled the approach of some yet unseen entity.

"Is it the snake?" Arthur asked, gripping the hilt of the crystal sword more tightly.

"No, not quite." Merlin sounded sure of that. "This is something else."

The footsteps grew closer. The sound only ceased when a hooded figure stepped out from behind one of the more well-endowed trees that lined the trail.

"Who goes there?" Reynold asked. His hand instinctively reached to draw his own sword from its sheath. He noticed the same murky miasma surrounding this individual.

"He was like us once," Merlin told them. "Except, I fear he ventured forth unprepared."

"What do you mean?" Arthur asked from behind.

"The forest has claimed him already." That knowledge saddened Merlin. Here stood another individual who fell to the influence of dark magic.

Just then, the hooded man lunged at them.

"Defend yourselves!" Merlin turned to see other cloaked figures emerging from the woods around them.

There was at least half a dozen. They each bore weapons forged from the woods themselves. As they rushed forward, long wooden pikes sought to skewer the heart of their prey.

Hayden struck first, heaving the ornate blade that seemed all but unwieldy. He cut down one of the dark-clad figures with a single downward stroke. His sword sliced the forest dweller clean in two. The spilt form tumbled to a heap on the ground, where it disintegrated and left only a loose pile of cloth in its wake. A pained screech filled the air, as the form of the slain withered away into nothing.

The others were locked in fights of their own.

Two hooded figures charged Merlin. He easily stopped their approach with the extending of the index finger on either hand. A bolt of fire shot forth and pierced each figure through the chest. The smell of charred flesh filled the air, and the flames spread through them, cracking and scorching their inhuman shape.

As the robes burned away, Merlin glimpsed the bodies beneath. Only a twisted husk of brittle wood in the shape of a man remained of the once human visage. The forest claimed them in more ways than one.

Another duo leapt forward in unison, hoping to catch Reynold unaware. He was ready for them. His blade flashed across the distance, cutting the throat of the first, before driving the point into the gut of the second—all in a single fluid motion.

It became immediately apparent that Reynold was the more skilled fighter among them. His eyes bore a keen awareness. Only past experience could contribute to those masterful combat skills.

Arthur, on the other hand, struggled in the face of their newest adversary. A single attacker perused him. He back peddled and stumbled into a sitting position on the ground. In the process of stumbling onto his hindquarters, Arthur unintentionally drove the point of the borrowed sword upwards. His hooded foe lunged forward, only to impale himself on Arthur's upturned blade. His fallen opponent dropped at his feet.

Where Reynold excelled at the flourish of swordsmanship, Arthur harbored an almost daunting amount of good fortune.

Watching that final exchange, Merlin shook his head. He wondered if they were actually cut out for the danger still ahead, but he knew they could no longer turn back. "We need to keep moving," he told them.

Reynold helped Arthur back onto his feet. "Should we not rest here a moment?"

"We cannot afford another ambush. We must keep moving." Merlin peered into the darkness on all sides, seeking any additional pursuers. He now suspected they were growing from the forest itself, out of the great misshapen trees, only disguising themselves as human servants.

"How are there so many of them?" Reynold asked, as they hastened from the site of battle.

"I know not," Merlin replied. "I may have misspoken in saying they were fallen men and women who took up arms against the evil residing here. I think they were birthed from the forest."

"Are you saying the forest is alive?" Arthur's mouth hung slightly agape.

Merlin chuckled at Arthur's blatant innocence. "All forests are alive, my boy. This one just happens to bear a grudge against mankind for some past transgression. I cannot say for sure what turned this place so evil, but it feels its secrets are threatened by our pilgrimage."

They were running now. The globe of light continued to mark the path ahead. Even now, they could hear followers hurrying through the forest after them. More attackers could spring forth at any moment.

The mouth of a cave appeared in front of them. The stench of death and decay wafted out from within its cramped enclosure.

Merlin froze, unprepared for the depravity he felt in that evil place. Its roots extended outwards in every direction, linking itself as the source of all troubles.

"What are you waiting for?" Arthur and Hayden were still moving toward the mouth of the cave.

Reynold felt it too. He stopped at Merlin's side. His ambitions crumbled in the face of that oppressive aura. "What is that place?" he asked Merlin.

"It's the heart of the darkness in these woods," Merlin explained, still struggling against his own growing uncertainty. "While beauty and goodness exist in this and all worlds, so too can be said for the opposite. Evil flourishes in places like these, where light cannot reach."

"How can we hope to face it?" Reynold's mind reeled.

The foot soldiers in the woods encircled them. Although out of sight, their movements could be heard in every direction.

Merlin's eyes slipped shut, entering a state of silent consideration. "We have a choice to make. We can turn back, but we will need to fight our way through the hordes of attackers that surround us, or we can press on and try to accomplish our original goal. We may die either way. I will let you choose your fate." He planted his feet, affirmed to remain until the boys settled their resolve.

Arthur surprised him, speaking for the entirety of their expedition: "We keep moving forward." Although sounding small in light of the potential consequences, a spark of determination punctuated his decision.

Merlin waited, expecting one of the elder brothers to speak in opposition, but each seemed to fall in line with Arthur's resolution. "Very well." Merlin clapped his hands together. An explosion of light accompanied the outward reverberation of sound. It blossomed, spread through the clearing, and permeated the surrounding wooded tapestry. The sound of approaching soldiers faded, as calm quiet replaced that of impending doom.

"You tricked us," Reynold accused, not sounding particularly perturbed. "Even if we chose to turn back, you could have seen us through with ease. Why not tell us that before?"

"I needed to gauge your determination." Merlin stepped toward the mouth of the cave. "We cannot hope to succeed in there if even the smallest doubt remains. I needed to know I could trust you. Will you still stand with me in this?"

The sincerity of Merlin's lie caught Reynold unsuspecting. A smile touched his lips.

Before the eldest brother could arrive at his answer, Arthur stepped forward. "I want to stand and fight." Choosing to see their endeavor through to its curtain call, the young and clumsy knight ascended to greater heights. In the end, Arthur would hold them together, even on the verge of collapse. This is his strength, and no one could hope to take that away from him.

Hayden clapped Arthur on the shoulder. He took his place at his brother's side. A hearty boom of laughter escaped the normally soft-spoken knight. Hayden would support his younger brother, even if death chased at their heels.

Only Reynold remained hesitant.

The sight of the cave made him quake in terror. Merlin offered the gift of magic, and now, that very same blessing stood to separate them. The thought of stepping over the threshold of that infested place maddened Reynold and drained his every ounce of strength. Yet, should he turn his back on them, he could never face his brothers or Merlin again. Even as every fiber of his being screamed against it, Reynold settled on a half-hearted decision. "Let's just get this over with."

Together, they stepped forth into the cave. The force within began playing tricks on them almost immediately. This, coupled with the increasingly potent stench, filled them with horrendous thoughts even more terrifying than what lay ahead.

Reynold's mind flashed to the moment their bodies would lay slain upon the ground. He watched himself and his brothers minced and slaughtered time and time again. They felt like memories of past experiences, as opposed to fabrications brought on by some dark enchantment. Over the course of his unraveling, the lines between reality and disillusion blurred into nonexistence.

"Don't let it in." Merlin's tone remained uncompromised, yet he knew of Reynold's struggle.

"But how did you know?" Reynold fought to ignore the visions, desiring a centralized focus on the here and now.

"I could see it all upon your face. Don't trust your mind; trust only your instincts." Merlin was beginning to sound more and more like a teacher.

"My head feels funny," Arthur remarked from behind. He lost his footing and braced himself against the surrounding wall.

Merlin acknowledged him with troubled eyes. "We're

passing through a barrier of sorts. We're very close now."

As if in response to his words, a roaring hiss billowed out from the depths of the cavern. The sound carried a concentrated dose of putrefied air.

They crept forward, seeking the source of that guttural clamor. They emerged into a large chamber. Streamlets of water crisscrossed from hairline cracks in the ceiling. Even as they tried to mask their approach, their boots squelched in the surrounding muck.

The Basilisk's nest made for an unsettling scene.

Arthur pressed a hand to his mouth at the sight of a mound of clearly human bones, piled almost as high as the ceiling.

The Basilisk stood more monstrous than originally described. The size of the inner cave allowed the beast to stand fully upright. With its back to them upon entering, its silver scales glimmered in the light of Merlin's emblazoned familiar; they displayed a distinctly metallic quality.

Merlin strode forward without any sign of fear. "Creature!" Merlin's voice boomed and echoed off the walls. "We have come to end your evil ways!"

The Basilisk spun to meet them, pitted eyes ablaze. It hissed and roared, sending a steady stream of spittle rained down around them. The thick globs sizzled and melted large chunks of stone upon making contact.

"Acid," Merlin remarked, with a touch of curiosity. "Do not allow any on your skin. It will burn right down to the bone." He sounded strangely untroubled. "I will protect you as best I can." He retrieved the vial of starlight from his vestment. Instead of anointing them with an extra coat of its blessing, he instead cast the glass enclosure at the ground. It shattered, and an array of lighted orbs scattered to the far corners of the cave.

Merlin next thrust his enclosed fist forward, as if planning to strike the Basilisk from afar. Upon his instruction, the surrounding fiery balls honed in on its scaly hide and exploded from every direction. The room was momentarily filled with a sudden, blinding brightness.

"Now!" Merlin exclaimed at once. "Attack now, while it is stunned!"

Reynold never hesitated either. He charged headlong with sword drawn.

Hayden followed close behind. His armor clamored against his larger frame, yet he managed to move with lumbering grace.

Arthur stayed by Merlin's side, watching as his elder brothers charged into battle. Merlin looked to him with a touch of contempt. "What are you waiting for?" he urged. "This is our only chance."

"I know..." Arthur sounded defeated before the battle had even begun.

Reynold and Hayden reached the Basilisk. It continued to writhe in pain, with eyes clamped shut, and tail waving wildly. Hayden swung once, bringing his oversized blade down with a hefty clang. The Basilisk's tail flew free of its body and landed several feet from its still struggling form. An inky fluid spread from the point of injury.

In the meantime, Reynold circled around to the beast's head. With sword clenched, he leapt into the air, arching the sharpened steel toward the Basilisk's defenseless face. He wanted to end this affair with a single blow.

However, in the Basilisk's pained throes, it ducked its head toward Reynold, catching him in flight. The iron-hardened skull of the snake struck him in the chest. He careened backwards and momentarily blacked out from the force of the blow; he struck pavement, awakening to a shooting pain in his lower back.

Even in its blinded state, the Basilisk never stopped fighting. It reared its head and spat a fresh torrent of acid in Hayden's direction. The armor-clad brother only barely managed to turn and use his back as a shield against the deadly downpour. It dissolved a large chunk of metal; another direct attack would surely see him reduced to bony scraps.

"Don't you dare." Back on his feet, Reynold refused to quit. Determined to reach his brother in time, he swung his sword at the serpent's broad body. No sooner did his blow connect, before the edge of his blade shattered without drawing even a single drop of blood.

The Basilisk turned with fangs bared. It moved with a quickness that made Reynold's graceful swordsmanship appear as nothing more than child's play. Looking up into the angular face of that otherworldly predator, he saw its eyes were keen and open once more.

They lost the opportunity Merlin afforded them.

Hayden prepared to launch a rescue attempt, but the creature foresaw his intentions. The Basilisk spun and jutted the remainder of its tail outwards, knocking Hayden off his feet. His sword fell to the ground at his side.

The Basilisk's jaw stretched wider; it moved to engorge Reynold. He had barely a moment to react. He dodged to the side and dropped to the ground in an attempt to roll to safety. He successfully evaded the first blow, but he could not hope to maintain this lucky streak.

"We need to do something." Arthur became enamored by a fearful frenzy.

"I've run through my magical supplies. The air of this place saps my strength." Merlin's eyes locked Arthur in their gaze. "You need to act or they will die. I gave you that sword for a reason. Use it!"

Arthur would have stayed frozen, if not for the sight of Reynold barely dodging another of the Basilisk's downward strikes. They were really going to die if Arthur failed to muster his courage.

All at once, without further consideration of the consequences, Arthur gripped the crystal sword by its hilt and raced to his brothers' aid. A powerful light radiated from the heart of the translucid artifact of a bygone world, and it intensified the more Arthur's resolve hardened in the face of certain demise.

As the Basilisk lashed out at Reynold once more, with mouth agape, Arthur stepped between them.

"Arthur, have you lost your mind?" Reynold accused from where he lay.

Arthur never heard those words. His body moved on its own, and the Basilisk recognized the threat of this newcomer a moment too late.

The blade glowed more fiercely now, illuminating even the darkest corners of the cave. Just as the snake opened its mouth, Arthur drove the blade straight and true. As the point pierced the back of the creature's throat, he could nearly feel the brush of its ivory fangs.

An almost human realization filled the Basilisk's eyes. Before it could think to snap its jaw shut around the boy's arms, the light of the crystal blade spread through its body. The scaly hide of the uncanny killer distorted and bulged outwards.

Casting aside his cowardly ways, Arthur stepped back and readied his sword for another attack. He became a shield for his eldest brother.

Instead of attacking, however, the Basilisk dropped to the floor of the cave. Its form continued to convulse, with the light coursing through its veins.

Behind the scenes, Merlin and Reynold witnessed a unique power struggle. The dark magic of the snake demon warred against the radiant magic birthed from the blade Excalibur—further intensified by Arthur's own courage and determination to save his brothers. As it happened, Arthur's light won the day, and eventually, the Basilisk lay still with eyes rolled back to white.

Merlin heaved a heavy sigh of relief. He half expected they would meet their end that day, but Arthur's strength proved more admirable than he ever anticipated. When bestowing Excalibur on the young knight, Merlin caught a hint of a deeper potential in the doe-eyed boy. It seemed fitting that the blade of legend would find its way into the hands of another who bore the name of its former master.

The brothers reconvened around Arthur, who seemed awestruck at knowing he felled the beast. Each of the older brothers embraced their younger sibling in turn, congratulating him on his victory, even as they were scolding him for placing himself in harm's way. They were torn between supporting his heroic endeavors and maintaining the protective guise of brotherly love.

"What in all the gods' names were you thinking?" Reynold hugged his brother more tightly.

"That was a true spectacle," Hayden remarked. The middle brother beamed with pride at their unexpected victory.

"Don't encourage him!" Reynold snapped, although he found himself smiling all the same.

Once their exchange had ended, the three brothers turned to where Merlin had previously been standing. They were surprised to find the old man was nowhere to be seen.

"Hey! Where did Merlin go?" Reynold called attention to the wizard's absence, sounding almost panicked by the revelation.

"He must have slipped out. Let's go after him." Arthur took off for the cave's exit at a sprint. They needed to at least thank Merlin for all he had done to help them and guide them on their way.

Plus, Arthur needed to return Excalibur as promised.

Outside, they found Merlin standing a short distance from the mouth of the cave. The landscape had changed completely. The forest no longer appeared dominated by the forces of darkness. With the threat of the Basilisk destroyed, a lush green bounty replaced nature's steady decay.

The brothers had never known the forest as anything other than cursed. No life could flourish there before, but now all those years of tyranny seemed swallowed in a wave of life blooming anew.

Only Merlin and Reynold recognized the magic spiraling in every direction.

"It's beautiful," Arthur remarked, unable to contain his fascination. "I don't think I've ever seen something this beautiful."

Merlin nodded in agreement, but held his tongue.

A powerful spirit lay dormant in those woods. That spirit had long been enslaved by the Basilisk's dark presence, but with the beast slain, the wellspring of the woods could flow once more. New life would flourish there, reaching the farthest corners of the world, until all the darkness had been driven back.

Something in the woods caught Merlin's attention. He set off at a brisk pace, seeking the source of the abnormality.

The brothers exchanged a curious glance, eventually following Merlin's lead. With sunlight trickling through the branches overhead, they no longer needed their lighted guide to show them the way.

Merlin stopped at the foot of a large tree.

The brothers stepped up around him. They were surprised to find the shape of a door carved into the bark of that peculiar tree. An intricate golden pattern, in the shape of a sunflower, shone upon the face of the door, while an intricate crystal knob protruded from one side.

Merlin turned and saw their shared fascination. He pushed his curiosity to the wayside for the time being. "I think this is where we must say our goodbyes."

"Where will you go?" Reynold asked, sounding troubled by their discovery.

"I think this was left here for me." Merlin looked longingly at the door. "This fight was only one of many. The darkness is still out there." Heaving a sigh, Merlin actually looked his age for the first time since first meeting those three extraordinary brothers. "I think fighting the darkness is what I'm meant to do. I've been doing it for so long that I hardly notice anymore, but I seem to have a knack for it."

The boys turned suddenly dour at the thought of going their separate ways.

Arthur broke from the collective. He held Excalibur up on level palms. "You said I needed to return it when we were done here."

Merlin stared for a long moment, transfixed by the crystal blade, before shaking his head slowly. "You were able to pull forth its power. It belongs to you now. Just promise to never use if for anything other than righteous intent. Its magic is pure and easily corrupted."

"I promise I'll only use it to help people." Arthur took hold of Excalibur once more, letting it drop at his side.

"Good, then I have no regrets leaving it in your care." Merlin seemed pleased by this.

Reynold pondered for a moment. "What if we came

with you instead?" A silence stretched between them. Although they considered the possibility, neither Hayden nor Arthur could bring themselves to voice this suggestion. "I guess we'd all have to agree to it, but we seemed to make a fairly good team this time around. Maybe we can help you fight the darkness."

Merlin smiled. That touched a part of his heart long cast in shadow. "I could never ask that of any of you. There's no telling where we might end up. You may never see your people again."

"I'm fine with that," Arthur forcefully interjected.

"You'd be leaving everything and everyone you've ever known. Are you saying you'd be okay with that?" Merlin seemed genuinely stunned.

"I wouldn't mind," Arthur admitted, never even stopping to consider the weight of those words. "It's for the greater good, right?"

"I couldn't ask that of you..."

"You don't have to." Hayden spoke next. "I think it's what we all want." His confession seemed the most unexpected of all.

The brothers shared a look, unspoken knowledge passed between them, and they each nodded in unison.

"It's decided then," said Reynold. "We're coming with you."

Merlin lowered his head in defeat. "Very well...I would gladly welcome your accompaniment." It had been a great many years since Merlin met anyone he liked quite as much as he liked those three brothers. He wanted to help them grow in new and wonderous ways, just as they wanted to assist in whatever the universe still had in store for him.

He turned back to the door. "Then shall we go?" Merlin asked the question. As he grasped the knob, a familiar thrum of magic filled his body.

The door opened, and they stepped forth into a lifetime of adventures.

Maple Mountain Lodge: A Compendium

Nestled amidst the highest peaks of the rarely ventured Maple Mountain sits a lodge of the same name. It bears a unique history unbeknownst to most. Traversing its many winding corridors, you almost feel a sense of foreboding mystery pulsing beneath the surface. The shadows here seem to convey a life of their own.

Venturing forth into the heart of this wintry refuge, many guests come seeking an escape from the world below. This place serves as a reality separate from the mundane regularity of society.

Even now, if you look hard enough, you will find any number of colorful characters squirreled away within its walls.

Isolated in a room on the third floor, a recently divorced man sits and conspires against the plight that so totally struck his peaceful life asunder. He considers his next move, never straying from thoughts of violence, as he takes one pull after the next from the dwindling contents of a carton of cigarettes laid out upon the bedside table. Just as the steady stream of smoke yellows the face of the surrounding cheaply plastered wallpaper, so too do his thoughts of envious vengeance stir a dark chord within the foundation of that underlying malevolence.

Their unheard tongue would rise in modest agreement, urging his hand toward the gun kept safely nestled at the bottom of his suitcase. The wench, who dared turn his love aside for the touch of another man, would soon learn the error of her ways. As acceptance gripped his resolve, a murmured consent radiated outward through the eaves of that hallowed place.

High upon those peaks, the Maple Mountain Lodge stands close to a precipice between this world and another close at hand. Should that other reality break through the thin barrier set to keep the forces of light and darkness separate, all things would come unraveled at the whim of the great cataclysm to follow.

That scorned man's hatred—and the violence it promised—would serve the greater workings of that dark intent.

Only a significant shift in the balance between good and evil could allow the door between worlds to open. The ruler of that far-off plane of existence would thank the malcontent in time, when his dreams were ultimately realized.

Elsewhere in those halls, where the sounds of small scurrying feet were chalked up to the old building settling on its foundation, other guests were wrought with troubles of their own.

On the top floor, a writer sits in an oversized armchair, peering out from his window, across the jagged mountain range. While running his fingertips through a tangle of beard, he considers the subject of his next bestselling novel. The solitude of the mountain helps him think; the view from on high spurs a wellspring of creativity. He feels sure that those seeds would soon grow into a masterpiece like nothing conceived before. This single stroke of genius would forever carve his name upon the mantle of the world.

In the end, the offspring of his time spent on Maple Mountain would grow to produce a hate-filled rhetoric. It would develop a dense following in the years to come, becoming the building blocks for a war that threatened to separate the nation. He would rise to lead that movement.

The day would come when the words conceived within those haunted halls would spell doom to many brave souls. From within the walls, voices seem to foreshadow that future, offering words of praise in that regard. They gave life to those dark thoughts, guiding his pen to inscribe words that blossomed out of hate and discrimination.

Their intentions were no secret. The war that would follow some years down the road would unshackle their king from his place of imprisonment, setting him free to seek vengeance upon those who allowed him to slip through the cracks into that desolate world.

The words of one writer, bent on seeing his name carried through the years, would conceive a battle hymn of endless horror. His name would go down in history, just not for the desired reason. Instead, he would become known as a hate monger and an enemy to all mankind. His influence would lay dormant for a time now, but by the end of the saga, he will bear the greatest sin of all.

The wheel started turning there. Atop Maple Mountain, a great tragedy would soon befall its occupants. A mystery long in the making would drive home a number of lingering questions.

Three doors down from the writer, a lonely, young woman buries her tear-soaked face in the comforting embrace of a pillow, all while considering her life choices. In her belly, unnoticed by any but her, a new life was growing without her consent. A senseless act of lust brought life to that miniscule being. Her assailant walked free, without a care in the world, while she was forced to carry this burden in secret.

She visited the Maple Mountain Lodge once prior, as a small girl in the accompaniment of her parents. They formed an ideal family, brimming with love and happiness; her life now seemed full of only pain and desperation. Trying to channel the warmth of her childhood, the time spent on that mountain arose as one of her fondest memories. She returned there, hoping to regain that which was stolen from her on the same night that man claimed her purity.

Yet, now that she was here, it all felt wrong. Its halls were teeming with the same essence of corruption that filled the sex addled minds of men seeking fresh prey to drive down into the pit of despair. She found something other than respite upon visiting the source of childhood reminiscence.

Once tied together, the bedding made for an effective noose. She hung it from an overhanging rafter. Now she only needed to talk herself up to the task at hand.

Of course, those unseen denizens of the deepest shadows sought to extinguish any doubt. They spoke of peace at the end of her long and arduous road, but only if she were to go through with it; otherwise, they promised her troubles would only continue to worsen.

She became a pendulum to mark the minutes. The makeshift noose held snug around her neck. A chair lay on its side at her feet. The life she grew to dread ended as surely as she hoped, but as the last light faded from her eyes, a dark splintering in the fabric of the world grew out of the void created in her absence.

The invasion grew ever closer now, urged onward with every successful infiltration.

Down in the lobby, a new family just arrived, with plans to spend the weekend basking in the sights of the mountain. They would embrace this opportunity to deepen their bonds, without even the slightest hint of realization at the consequences to be paid for their choice of travel destination. One of their own would serve as a catalyst in matters yet untold.

The young daughter peers about with a wide-eyed sense of wonder. She would later wake screaming from a nightmare, in which strange black creatures tried to drag her parents away to some dark place beyond even her wildest imaginings. The dream would frighten her, but her parents would reassure her that no such calamity would befall them.

How wrong they were.

Checking into the lodge now, the desk clerk looks from husband to wife, with a glistening smile set to welcome them. The couple talks excitedly. They sign some paperwork, making record of their credit card information, while the clerk runs down the list of necessities before passing two room keys their way.

They would be staying on the fourth floor, and they would have the floor all to themselves.

As they gather their luggage and head upstairs, the elderly gentleman working the front desk returns his attention to a news magazine. The cover showcases the face of a man then described as "Family Man Turned Lunatic." The full article recounts the shocking transformation of a seemingly ordinary working man into a cold-blooded killer. He started off murdering his wife and newborn son, before embarking on a spree of carnage.

His name—before losing himself entirely to the madness—was Trevor Thompson. Now, he was just another of the fallen.

In acknowledgement to this bit of news, you might imagine you can almost hear a knowing laughter emanating in the air. Those dark beings, hidden amidst the shadows, considered this one of their finest accomplishments.

The walls between the worlds are beginning to crumble now. A dark tide hides in wait just out of sight. The stage is set for the next act in this otherworldly showstopper.

Maple Mountain Lodge stands at a pivotal point on the edge of the balance. One wrong move could send it cascading over the edge. Many tales in the saga find their start here, as the Emperor of the Night sits atop his throne, somewhere out amidst the ruined fields of Destination.

Dawn

"Wake up!" I screamed those words inside my head, hoping they would sink in and become something more tangible.

They don't. They never do. No matter how much I insist upon escaping the prison that is my own body, it never heeds my words. I wish to be free once more, but instead I lie here, drifting slowly into oblivion.

A bright white light surrounds me. It fills everything to overflowing. This whiteness is like watching the sun rising on the horizon over and over again. It never ends. It just keeps going.

Something happened to me, landing me in this place. I don't know what happened, but I know it was something serious.

I feel myself floating above the world. My body hangs just out of reach in the whiteness beneath me. My physical form stays drifting through the expanse, while my mind roars with an intense desire for release.

How long have I been here? Time no longer holds any semblance of meaning.

How much longer will I stay? The answer alludes me no matter how hard I try to awaken from this dreamscape.

Sometimes voices drift in from through the veil. It's usually the voice of one of the many doctors or nurses, seeing that my physical form retains its lively nature.

Occasionally, those voices belong to my friends and family members. Their words are soft and reassuring. In turn, they each tell me how much they love me and wish to see me back among the living.

I wonder about that though...

In life, I always felt alone...Those same people visiting me on the outside were never there for me when both my body and soul were still connected, yet now they find themselves troubled by my absence.

At one point, I started thinking it best for all of this to end. When such thoughts happen to cross my mind, the radiance that surrounds me would start to fade, until those thoughts retreated back behind my own cowardice. It seems I can only maintain my consciousness in this plane for as long as I will myself to carry on.

I find myself determined to prove dominant in regards to my life. This world—no matter how cruel and heartless it may be—will not take me.

In life, I tended to walk a more downtrodden path, riddled with self-doubt and condescension. I never believed I would amount to much, so I often took the easy way out...The struggle always seemed like too much work.

Now, I'm choosing to strive for something. It took a near death experience to make me realize how much I cherished that simple life. My eyes were open now, and the light shone more brightly than ever.

I took that light for granted...

It happened unexpectedly. All at once, the light that sustained my continued existence flickered out. A cold darkness quickly rushed in to blanket everything.

I don't know what happened to trigger that sudden change in perception. I find myself struggling to see through the filmy haze lingering across my field of vision. I watched as my body—my real body—drifted off into the abyss. It felt lost to me now, severing my only connection to the world outside of here.

How long did I spend there in the dark? No longer able to see, I found myself growing very afraid of what may come next.

Bracing myself against the possibility that the end was growing nearer, I became one with that darkness, melding and shifting to contort myself to this new environment. I felt myself being carried off somewhere...

A coldness spread its fingers over my skin...It continued its advance until the feeling reached every inch of my person.

Wait...This isn't right...

I couldn't remember the last time I genuinely *felt* anything. I could remember trying to summon the memory of sensation, but now I was actually feeling, and it was like a series of ice-cold razor blades jittering to life upon my skin.

My eyes seemed unresponsive at first, but I focused intently on forcing them to open, and eventually they did. It's an arduous task, trying to get muscles that have lain dormant for so long to respond, but my willpower proved superior. I'm momentarily blinded by a pair of florescent lights hanging overhead. This light was somehow more real than the light that surrounded me in that absent prison. I was looking through eyes that hadn't looked upon the world in quite some time, and they felt dry and filled with sand. Soon, they would start feeling like my eyes again, but just then, they felt strange and alien.

I woke from an instant of blind panic. One minute, I felt certain my life was drawing to a close, but in reality, it only presented itself as a side-effect of my journey back to the land of the living.

Lying in a hospital bed, still recuperating from a yet undisclosed ordeal, I found myself returning from the pinnacle of death. I spent a prolonged period of time drifting through a void of hopelessness, only to return to life renewed.

The hustle and bustle started around me then. Faces blurred passed and seemed to fuse together. In those moments, as I remembered the feel of the darkness closing around me, I pledged to never forget the fear I encountered there.

In the days and weeks to come, the memory of the void would fade slowly...Soon, I would remember only the darkness, but that was ok. It would hold me together and help me become a more complete person.

03/19/2019

Made in the USA
Middletown, DE
26 March 2019